Stella Stands Alone

Also by *A. LaFaye*

Worth, winner of the Scott O'Dell Award
for Historical Fiction

Stella Stands Alone

A. LaFAYE

SIMON & SCHUSTER BFYR

NEW YORK   LONDON   TORONTO   SYDNEY

SIMON & SCHUSTER BFYR

An imprint of Simon & Schuster Children's Publishing Division
1230 Avenue of the Americas, New York, New York 10020

For information about special discounts for bulk purchases, please contact Simon & Schuster
Special Sales at 1-866-506-1949 or business@simonandschuster.com.
The Simon & Schuster Speakers Bureau can bring authors to your live event.
For more information or to book an event, contact the Simon & Schuster Speakers Bureau at
1-866-248-3049 or visit our website at www.simonspeakers.com.
Also available in a Simon & Schuster Books for Young Readers hardcover edition.
Book design by Karen Hudson
The text of this book was set in Fairfield LH.
Manufactured in the United States of America
First Simon & Schuster Books for Young Readers paperback edition February 2010
2 4 6 8 10 9 7 5 3 1
The Library of Congress has cataloged the hardcover edition as follows:
LaFaye, A.
Stella stands alone / A. LaFaye.—1st ed.
p. cm.
Summary: Fourteen-year-old Stella, orphaned just after the Civil War, fights to keep her
family's plantation and fulfill her father's desire to turn land over to the people who have
worked on it for generations, but first she must find her father's hidden deed and will.
ISBN 978-1-4169-1164-7 (hc)
1. Reconstruction (U.S. history, 1865–1877)—Juvenile fiction. 2. Southern States—
History—1865–1877—Juvenile fiction. [1. Reconstruction (U.S. history, 1865–1877)—
Fiction. 2. Swindlers and swindling—Fiction. 3. Orphans—Fiction. 4. Conduct of life—
Fiction. 5. Freed men—Fiction. 6. African Americans—Fiction. 7. Reconstruction (U.S.
history, 1865–1877)—Fiction. 8. Southern States—History—1865–1877—Fiction.]
I. Title.
PZ7.L1413SSe 2008
[Fic]—dc22
2007038725
ISBN 978-1-4169-8647-8 (pbk)
ISBN 978-1-4169-7496-3 (eBook)

Contents

To all those who fight for equality

Acknowledgments

I want to thank David Gale, Alexandra Cooper, Dr. Wilma King, Nikki Grimes, Dr. Dianne Johnson, and Pan Muñoz Ryan for all of their hard work, guidance, and support in bringing this to print. Thank you, Marcia, for your continued support. And I am eternally grateful for the gifts God has given me that have allowed me to create this book.

Wishful Thinking

A Note from A. LaFaye

You've heard of historical fiction, but you may not know about "alternate history," which is a special category of historical fiction. These novels take historical events and alter them to see how history would've changed as a result. Most of these novels change something pivotal. In *The Year of the Hangman* by Gary Blackwood, George Washington is assassinated by the British, so the colonies never win their independence.

But some "alternate history" novels change a small thing in history to look at what might have been possible if everyday folks had done things differently. Sherley Williams does that by having two historical women, who never met in real life, meet on the pages of her novel *Dessa Rose*. In the book, a courageous young woman who escaped a slave coffle only to be killed for the crime in real life, escapes this fate in fiction and meets up with a white slave owner who harbored escaped slaves because she had no other way to keep the place running after her husband abandoned her on their remote plantation. These two women team up with the slaves on the plantation to start a con game to raise enough money to buy their own land out West. They have the plantation owner pretend to sell the slaves, then break the slaves out of bondage only to move on and sell them again. This novel takes a look at one of the possible things that could've happened if African Americans and European Americans had crossed the boundaries of slavery and prejudice to work together.

After reading this powerful novel for adults, I wanted to take a similar approach in a book for young readers. The novel you're about to read is my own piece of alternate historical fiction that asks what could've happened if the people of the South had worked together to fight for what would've been owed to African Americans in a just world.

Stella Stands Alone

The Warning
May 1866

Even from my perch on the roof of Daddy's old office, I could only see a bit down the road on account of all the gnarly old oaks crowding in on both sides. So I didn't see the rust red of Mr. Daniel Richardson's vest until he came within shouting distance, and that's just where he stopped.

Stood there holding a hanky up to his mouth like the yellow fever that killed my mama might just fly out there and snatch him dead. "That you up there, Stella Reid?" he shouted.

I'm not one for idle talk, so I didn't bother answering.

"I've come to give you notice." He yelled so hard, his voice went scratchy. "The bank owns Oak Grove as of this morning. The property will be sold at auction. You have two weeks to pack your things and move on to your cousin Mertle's. Be sure to smoke that fever out of the house before you go."

He didn't even say "*your property*" because that suggested I had some claim to the land my family had owned since my great-granddaddy decided to try his hand at growing cotton back when them rabble rousers met in Philadelphia to start a revolution against them British.

It's all on account of we still couldn't find Daddy's will and the deed he kept with it. Mama and I had searched from the floorboards to the treetops for them papers, but found nothing. Not even the payment book that proved Daddy done paid every last penny for the land he bought from our neighbor Hendersen before he died. Then the bank started saying Daddy didn't pay down all the interest. Wouldn't give me no chance to pay it off myself. Said it's too long overdue now that Daddy's been gone near to a year. Not that they said one word on the matter before they sent us that foreclosure.

Richardson's the one who did all that falsifying. And you can bet on a Bible that he'll be the top bidder at that auction he'd been going on about. That man's had his eyes on Oak Grove since the day he opened them. All on account of the fact my great-granddaddy done bought the land from Richardson's granddaddy in a deal the Richardson clan called shady because the land they sold done produced more cotton than the land they'd kept. Now that old Richardson thought he had some kind of claim on the place. He wanted every last Reid off the land. Wouldn't even put it past him to be moving the people in the Reid family plot if he got his hands on Oak Grove. Why, he hadn't even waited an hour past the dawn of the third day after we buried my mama. Man had evil in his bones.

"Did you hear me, Stella Reid?"

My silence makes folks yell louder. Might be that believing I'm hard of hearing is easier to swallow than the offense of being ignored.

"Miss Reid?"

I began to think he might pop a vocal cord like a fiddle string. I decided to wait and see if such a thing could happen.

But he just shouted, "You've been warned." Then he walked off down the road.

Duly noted, you old coot, but I'd been eager to hear him bust a vocal cord. Then again, I might get that opportunity the next time we met. Old Man Richardson tended to do a lot of shouting around me.

Felt good to have him gone. Like a bad storm carried south toward the gulf, so it could just run out of wind over the ocean somewhere. Too bad such a storm couldn't take him out to sea.

I turned around for a look-see at Oak Grove, letting my eyes wander from Mama's resting place among the Reids sleeping under their grass blankets on the wooded hill due north to the tidy brick rows of the folks' quarters along the road headed south to the meeting house. I could near about smell the cotton growing in the summer sun.

A place soaks up its history. Things that happen there seep into the bricks of the houses and sift down into the soil of the fields, becoming permanent to anybody who could see the signs. My mama'd forever be in the garden where she laid down her own pathways in stones she quarried from the creek bed herself. My daddy'd never leave the stables where he'd carved the name of each horse into the stall doors. Mr. Beeman left his mark in the blacksmith's shop, working his own family sign to hang over the door. Wasn't an inch of Oak Grove that didn't speak of the past. That's why I could never leave it. I could hear and see those folks as if they never left. Who would tell of them with me gone?

Daniel Richardson could holler till the devil told him to pipe down. I'd never leave my home place. Never walk away from all that my family and the folks did to make this plantation fit enough to envy up the likes of Daniel Richardson.

The law may say I didn't own the land, but that same law used to say the people who worked this land were nothing more than my daddy's property. The Lord knows you can't own another person. And He's as much as told me He meant for me to keep Oak Grove—not for myself mind you, but for the people who really owned the place.

Got families on this land that been working it since a Reid laid claim to the place. And I say working 'cause Daddy done paid those folks a wage since Granddaddy passed on back when I wasn't much more than a bawling baby. And Oak Grove is my world. A place where things run a little different. A bit more to the Lord's liking, in my way of thinking.

Since Daddy started running things, folks here got a living wage for their work. Most are saving up to buy their own land, but to do that they had to move away from Helensburg on account of the laws here say no black man can own property. Now, Yankee law throws that evil old law down the well. But you can't sell the planters in these parts on that idea.

That's why so many of the folks of Oak Grove stayed on, worked the place their family been working. Why the Winfields got them three generations buried down past the rock bed. Their kin and everyone who took a hoe to this soil have a claim on it. Daddy thought that way and meant to make it legal, but his mama wouldn't sign no papers to turn it over, saying weren't no black man going to own *her* land until they put her in the ground. And she weren't the only one giving Daddy trouble.

Why, Daddy couldn't do nothing on Oak Grove that went against the way of things without seeing blood run. The planters in these parts been breaking my Daddy down since I had a mind to know what's what. They had a law saying freedmen couldn't live in these parts, but Daddy still tried to give the folks of Oak Grove their freedom even before the war. Them planters fought like demons to keep things as they liked them.

Daddy'd pay for free papers on a body only to have Hendersen or Richardson or some other rich son of an evil planter send out a lying notice that said he owned the poor man who weren't nothing but a runaway. Hunted that fella down like a dog, burning his freedom papers, then worked him to the bone right where Daddy could see him. Driving that poor man so hard to punish him for thinking he could be free.

Daddy tried to buy the men back to Oak Grove, but them planters just laughed at him, sending him to seething so bad I thought he'd tear his office to the ground, smashing things and breaking windows, cursing till the devil sat up to listen.

But Daddy kept trying. Sent folks under the cover of night on the railroad with no tracks that led north to freedom and land of their own. But Daddy couldn't do it fastlike or the planters in these parts would get wise and turn their sights on the people of Oak Grove again, threatening fire or accidents like the blade that nearly took Daddy's foot off when he tried to buy him a new thresher the day he sent Granddaddy's carpenter, Mr. Parker, north, or the grain hatch opening up on Grady Tanbridge the morning before he planned to take the railroad out of town, or the Nelson twins drowning in the creek before their mama could take them to meet up with their daddy, who'd reached Ohio that spring.

A. LaFaye

The folks on Oak Grove had stepped into a deadly dance with the planters here in the Natchez district, each one trying to fool the other into thinking they hadn't missed a step. Our people dancing real prettylike, hoping nobody could see the one we tried to shuffle off the dance floor to freedom.

But the planters in these parts had their eyes fit to bore through your soul. They caught on to too many things. No matter how careful we stepped, they usually showed up to cut off our toes. And Richardson had him a right sharp knife, ready to cut away all of Oak Grove this time. And I had nothing but prayer and a promise standing between me and that blade.

If I had the power, I'd sign all of us onto the deed of Oak Grove, make it legal—a match to what the Lord knows to be true. Those who work the land own it by just rights. They'd be taking what's owed them by my reckoning. Ain't no one going to move me or the folks who work it off Oak Grove.

But Richardson's been trying to do it for years. When Daddy died, Richardson started coming round to talk Mama into selling. She'd answered him with a shotgun blast over his head and a demand to have her squatter's rights till she could find the deed and be legal. He'd scurry off into the woods like a scared little rabbit, shouting back, "You find your papers. I'll find mine."

Never knew what he meant until he came a calling about a foreclosure. Yellow fever took Mama from this world, so now Richardson wanted me to pack my things and move into town with Cousin Mertle, like our family hadn't bought the land from his generations ago. Well, he'd be waiting for the Mississippi to freeze in New Orleans before I packed anything more than his empty threats. I planned on staying there on the land to which I was born.

Hattie Comes, Carting a Problem

"Stella!" My friend Hattie's voice turned me around. "What you doing sitting on the roof like a rooster?"

"Just seeing." I turned my feet to the east, slid down the roof to jump onto the wood pile, then pushed off for a nice landing on the mossy edge of the flower bed.

"Girl!" Hattie shouted.

I just laughed at her. She followed me as I headed to the kitchen, saying, "It's true what they say about you, you are *touched* in the head."

Heading into the kitchen, I gave a nod to Mrs. Bishop, who had every woman to call herself a cook working to get the noon meal ready before they rang the bell to call folks in from the fields. I slipped in to grab me some of her perk-up-your-tongue salted pork.

"Did you hear me? Touched, I tell you. Jumping around like some monkey."

Folks always went on about my peculiar ways, but I'd gotten so's I didn't even hear their judgment talk anymore. And if Hattie didn't have anything better to say, I planned on ignoring her, too.

Mrs. Wynston, strongest woman ever to put hand to broom, pushed a plate under my hand and tapped the bread with her spoon, but I didn't pay her any more mind than I did Hattie.

"Don't you go clamming up on me, Miss Stella!" Hattie followed me outside. "I got to talk to you.

"Hendersen say he got a paper say he can work me legal, but won't let me read it. Got all spitting when I tried." She shook her head to knock a memory loose, then put on Hendersen's growl of a voice, saying, "Darkie, who you learn that reading from?"

Hands on her hips, words red and hot like fire, Hattie said, "He forget he don't own me no more?"

That Hendersen had a dried-up peach for a brain. Hattie done learned to read sitting right next to me. Back then, her mama, Miss Rosie, done the sewing for Mama and Mrs. Hendersen. We studied reading on the days Miss Rosie came to Oak Grove until that sour old woman started saying Miss Rosie made prettier dresses for Mama and threatened to cut Miss Rosie's hair clean off her head if she sewed one more thing for Mama.

After that, Hattie had to sneak out of her duties over at the big house on the Hendersen plantation to come see me. But with the anger she had spewing out like sparks, it's a good thing for the Hendersens that she didn't stay there.

Didn't need to ask her about that paper she'd been going on about—she'd come around to it again. Didn't take but the blink of an eye.

"Said with Mama and Papa gone, I'm his to claim. Says I'm an orphan. I ain't no orphan!" She pointed. "You see any gravestones with my mama's name on it?"

"Hattie!" Mrs. Bishop leaned out the kitchen door, waving a

knife like a wand. "Don't go tempting the devil, now!"

"Sorry, Mrs. Bishop."

"Save your words for the Good Lord."

Mrs. Bishop didn't take to no dark talk, said it put ideas in the devil's head. That fool ain't got no head. Evil rotted it clean off by now, I'm sure.

Hattie set to pacing. "Hendersen has one of them papers on all of Miss Clara's girls on account of their daddy dying over in Vicksburg."

Folks said him a mighty fine funeral at the river for fighting under Old Glory to help General Grant take Vicksburg. But it seemed a shame to leave Miss Clara to raise all seven of them girls by her ownself.

"And Granny Quinna's boys. Them too. And Royce and Paddy. Near to twenty of us young'uns. Can he do that? Sign us up to work till we grown? Ain't got to pay us nothing, he say. Not a cent. Say we orphans and got to rely on his charity to keep us fed and clothed." She pulled on her dress. "My mama done put this dress on my back and my papa done killed the cured rabbit I ate for my supper last night. Which I ate in my own house and cooked my own self. How can he call me an orphan?"

Now when Hattie got to ranting, didn't matter that I never said much, she said enough for a whole church full of people.

"Sure, Mama been gone for a bit. But you can't find no children you lost just by turning over some rock. She got searching to do. Searching."

Miss Rosie had her three sons down in Mobile before she got sold away to Hendersen. With freedom on her side now, she could find them. But the search had kept her away for weeks at a time.

9

When she'd come home, she'd look all thin and red-eyed, like she done beat the bushes from Mobile to Natchez to find those boys. I prayed she did, for she couldn't be whole without them.

"And if that Hendersen hadn't turned every planter in these parts against my papa, he wouldn't have to be up there in Natchez making furniture for those Yankees. He'd be here with us, selling enough furniture in these parts to get us to Philadelphia."

Mr. Caleb, Hattie's daddy, made furniture fit for selling to the Queen of England. Like she needed anything more than a good swift kick in the behind. But still, he could make furniture so fine you'd think he'd trained under the Lord Jesus himself. I do wonder what kind of furniture the Lord made.

"Stella!" Hattie stomped on my foot. "You're wandering again. I can see it in your eyes. This is serious!"

Hattie had it right. Planters in these parts had built up the fires of their wickedness because they knew the Yankee tax man was coming. They had all that land to pay for and no money to speak of. Fighting a war's an expensive thing. Now they'd turned to stealing children for free labor to make ends meet.

"He got that paper saying I can't leave till I'm grown. I know Mama and Papa won't leave me." Hattie looked ready to spout tears. "We'll never get to his brother in Philadelphia."

Felt the guilt of it sting me, but I liked that idea right well. Not the signing the paper part, but the staying part. I'd called Hattie friend since we messed ourselves as babies, so I hated the idea of her leaving, but I didn't want her hurt none either.

"Mr. Caleb'll work around it."

"You say that like it's driving a wagon around a tree in the road. It's a legal paper and that Hendersen's gonna lock me up until I promise to do the work."

"Call your folks home."

"Don't you think I tried? Sent word through everyone headed in the right direction. Even thought of tying notes to the legs of crows. What more can I do?" Hattie shook her head. "That Hendersen wants to own the world like every other fat-bellied planter. I wish they'd all get yellow fever and die."

Just the mention of that awful sickness made me swoon, seeing my mama shriveled up and crying in her bed, "Just a sip, Stella, just a sip."

All she wanted was water. Why couldn't they just give her water? The Good Lord had her name in His book. No need to make her suffer on her way to meet Him. Didn't matter to me what no doctor said about sweating out no poison. I figured we should just give her the darn water and let her go.

I sat down, hating the tears on my cheek for being there.

Hattie appeared beside me. "I'm sorry, Stella, but those awful men deserve it. Your mama didn't." She gave me a hug.

Mama couldn't be happier now, being part of heaven's host and seeing Daddy again. She just shouldn't have had to suffer like that. But even then, Mama had been thinking on other folks rather than herself. No one who hadn't fought that fever and won, like Mrs. Wynston, could even go into the house. And it worked, too. That fever never spread to the folks. I was supposed to stay away, but I snuck in while she slept. Toward the end, she didn't even have the strength to shoo me no more. I figured the fever couldn't touch me if it hadn't already. As that evil sickness took my mama away day by day, I grew to see it as an evil thing to be hated. Just wished I could've found me a way to hunt it down and kill it.

But that evil fever had gone and given me what little time I had to find a way to keep Oak Grove. Richardson kept his distance for fear of catching it. He gave me two weeks to let the house air out, ordering me around like I was nothing more than a house girl fetching his slippers.

Well, I'd fetch them right down his throat if he wasn't careful. But I'd be a liar if I didn't say all his yelling and threatening didn't have me nervous enough to set to praying right then and there. Not just for me and the folks of Oak Grove, but also for Hattie and her family. *Show us the path, Lord. Show us the path.*

The Path

I've always been one to follow my own path—cutting through the woods while most people take the road, using an open window rather than a door, sitting on a roof 'stead of a porch. Most folks thought I did it to be contrary, but really, I followed my mind. Did what felt natural to me, not what folks said I should do.

Take talking, for instance. Never said a word as a wee child. People cooed at me, chanting "say this" or "say that" all livelong day. But I didn't see no call for saying what I didn't mean. When I's about three, I followed Mama out to the garden and a snake came right in for a look-see. If Mama didn't catch sight of him, she'd a turned too quick and he'd a bit her, so I said, "Mama, you got a snake on your tail."

Mama turned, cut that snake in half with her hoe, then stared up at me like I'd done killed it myself. "Stella, you spoke."

Who wouldn't speak with a poisonous snake slithering up on her mama?

I didn't see no cause for celebration, but Mama whooped and hollered, pulled me up into a hug, then ran me to Daddy, asking could I tell him what I'd said. There being no snake around, I didn't see no reason to repeat it, so I held my tongue.

I do that most days. As I figure it, folks spend a good bit of their time talking about things that don't matter none except for the noise of it all. I figure words for something useful, so I just use my words when I got something important to say. Seems right peculiar to most folks on account of me being silent so much, but I've found when you aren't talking, you hear a lot more. Like God Himself. Most folks said me hearing the Lord weren't natural, even called it evil. But I never did follow the regular path to God.

Most folks say churchgoing and Bible reading are the ways to obey the Good Lord. May God punish me if I'm wrong, but I never did figure it that way. I'd been to church with my mama, heard those Bible-reading folks go on about how the "Good Book," as they called it, said that colored folks were meant to be slaves on account of them being evil and soulless. If you ask me, you'd have to be without a soul to beat a man to death for stealing meat to feed his family or stringing a woman up in a tree for trying to run free with her babies. No sir, there's no goodness there. And the God I know would brand them people who could do such things as evil sinners.

I couldn't sit in that building with those people knowing what they did when they went home. And any book they'd use to defend their ways didn't need to be read by my account. Mama shook her head and patted her chest when I said such things, like I'd taken her breath away. She'd say, "Now, Stella, no one is free of sin. Least of all unruly little girls with ideas too big for their wee heads. You have no right to be placing yourself above others like that. You should be sitting in church side by side with all the other sinners. For every sin is equal in the eyes of the Lord."

God may see sin that way, but I ain't got that big of a heart. No sir, I keep my distance from those sinful folks and their evil ways. For services, I get me a spot in a good tree by the creek and listen in to the preaching and the singing and the testifying of the colored folks they don't allow in that church Mama done dragged me to.

But most days, I go straight to the well for my time with God, praying to the Good Lord himself. They can say I'm touched. They can say I'm a heathen and a liar all they want. But I believe the words the Good Lord tells me when I pray. Now, I don't hear the Lord's voice like a man whispering in my ear. It's more like a message carried on the wings of a feeling—a deep-down warmth-in-my-soul kind of sureness. I know it's right straight down to the last drop of blood in my body.

When I walked to the garden one afternoon and saw how Mama'd taken to wiping her brow and clearing her throat, looking a shade like the hearts of the daisies she tended, I recognized the signs of yellow fever and I set to pray, saying, "Dear Lord, please don't take my mama."

But the Lord said, "She'll be traveling soon."

His words had me gripping that garden fence so hard I near about bled.

"Mama," I said, wanting to warn her, to beg her to stay.

"Yes, Stella?" Mama always looked up when I called, on account of the fact I hardly ever spoke, so when I did folks figured I had something special to say.

And I did. I sure did. But the Lord told me, "She'll be traveling to me."

Then I knew I had no right to deny Mama the chance to be with the Lord who made her. Besides, Mama never did take to me hearing the Lord in my head. Said it wasn't natural.

Even heard her whispering about it to Mrs. Wynston one morning while they made up the bed in my room with me hiding under it. I favored such a spot on linen day: Gave me a chance to listen in on what Mama was thinking about me.

"I fear it might be a sign of the devil, Casadine," Mama said, tucking in a corner.

Mrs. Wynston clucked her tongue. "Folks be seeing the devil in any old thing they can't understand."

"But Violet Stevenson said . . ."

Mrs. Wynston stood up, then said, "You think I'm the devil?"

"Of course not, Casadine. If you were to go first, I'd expect you to be greeting me at the gates of heaven."

"Well, thank you, Miss Gayle Anne." Mrs. Wynston went all smiles and softness. "But that Violet Stevenson you been talking about says I'm devil-born on account of my remedies."

"Huh," Mama barked. "My husband still has two legs on account of your remedies."

Mama spoke true. A snake bite swelled Daddy's leg up like a pig bladder balloon—all black with venom. Dr. Aaronson said the best thing for Daddy would be to cut off the leg before the poison reached his heart. Mama just thanked him for his advice and sent him on home. Then Mrs. Wynston cooked her up a remedy that smelled like the insides of a dead dog, but it pulled that poison right out.

Mrs. Wynston snapped a pillowcase into Mama's leg, saying, "Well then, don't go trusting anything that Stevenson woman says about the devil. If you ask me, she's the one with the devil whispering in her ear, the way she talks about our Stella."

Mama smiled. "I did ask you and now I have to thank you for making me feel a whole lot better."

They both laughed and set to putting down the quilt, chatting on about this and that. Felt like looking into the future and seeing Hattie and I come our mama days. Now, the laws of the land say such a bond can't be between a white woman and a black woman, but such laws don't have much play here on Oak Grove.

Before they left the room, Mama said, "Stella still worries me."

"Miss Gayle Anne, you keep those worries of yourn so close, you'll be loath to give them over to St. Peter when he asks for them at the gates of Heaven."

Mama let out a fake cry of fear, then said, "Oh, my, do you think so?"

They left the room laughing and I had to scoot over for a peek. Mrs. Wynston turned as she closed the door and gave me a wink. I never could hide a thing from that woman.

Nowadays, the Lord's voice is as clear as ever. And I do my best to listen when the Lord speaks to me. When I prayed on what would happen to Oak Grove after Mama died, the Lord said as clear as a mockingbird come morning, "Oak Grove will be under your feet until I call you home."

And I'm not one to doubt the Lord when it comes to solving a body's problem, so when Hattie brought me a problem of her own, I set to praying. The Lord told me to get myself on a horse and down to Potter's Creek to find Miss Rosie, so that's just what I did.

Isaac, Jacob, Abraham

Potter's Creek runs through a clearing fit for meeting about fifteen miles south of Helensburg. Colored folks around those parts gathered there to call on the Lord and sing and pray. Had to do it deep in the woods real privatelike because them falsifying would-be-God-lovers who owned the plantations didn't allow coloreds to have no church meetings.

Come the end of the war, folks who took to sharecropping put their houses up around that clearing and built them a church and a school there. It's a bit of a town now. Even got them a small store for selling a little a' this and a little a' that, but they can't put no sign up because the planters in these parts like their sharecroppers to buy on credit at the local store. Meaning them greedy grubs like to steal a hard worker's money before they get it.

Well, Miss Rosie been known to stop off at Potter's Creek coming to and from her searching trips. Seemed just right when the Lord told me to find her there. And I figured I would, so I saddled me up a horse and headed to her directly. Night come before I seen the creek snaking under the road and knew to turn into the trees.

Cut through the trees to reach the Winfrey place where Miss Rosie stayed, on account of her being friends with Miss Mavis Winfrey.

Tied my horse to their porch post, then knocked.

Gave Miss Mavis a bit of a start. "Sorry, didn't expect to see no white face at my door at this hour."

Her saying "white face" dropped a rock into my heart. Making me feel small and wrong for not being one of her people. But I had Miss Rosie to find.

Miss Mavis said, "You be Stella, right?"

I nodded.

"Come on in. Rosie's in a bad way."

For a bit, I thought she'd taken sick, but seeing Miss Rosie rocking in the chair by the window, her eyes fierce and staring, her hands gripping the chair's arms like they might disappear beneath her fingers, I knew the memories had her.

Her words just pouring out like she thought they could fill the room and hold her together. "Isaac, Jacob, Abraham. Isaac had him gray eyes like his daddy. Jacob had that broken tooth from the fall outta that tree. Abraham, but a baby. Just a baby child. He smelled like hickory. Isaac, Jacob, Abraham."

I'd seen Miss Rosie like this but once before, when a cut on Hattie's arm turned evil sick and nearly took that poor girl from this world. That night, Miss Rosie took to chanting about the boys she'd lost. And weren't nothing Mr. Caleb could do, just had to let her talk it out. Tell it through.

And that's just what I had to do. I stood by the door and listened.

"Was a Saturday," she said, gripping that arm till her knuckles

19

looked ready to bust. "Had ham stew cooking in my head. Come fall, Master Turner always give us ham on Saturdays. Made stew to give us all enough to eat.

"Day hadn't even shaken the night out of his coat when I come down the road, sewing under my arm. Miss Turner never did like me bringing my babies into the shop, so I's coming back from leaving my Abraham with Granny Ulysses when I sees Rafferty coming down the hill. No overseer come down that hill after the hands go to the fields 'lessen someone took sick, so I turns around to see who got the cloth on they door.

"'Rosie,' he say, making me jump. Why he talking to me?

"'Rosie,' he say again. 'We have to go. Get your things.'

"'I got my things,' I told him, holding up the sewing I done for Miss Turner. Made her a right nice dress for the garden party at the Benson place. Had gray glass buttons. I remember 'cause they always make me think of my boy Isaac. He had gray eyes, like my man Earl. Gray as the stones leading to the river. Even thought of running there, jumping in and swimming. I could hide out at the Piminger place till Earl could reach me. We'd run. Run with them boys. Keep to the river so's the dogs couldn't track us. We's always talking how we'd run.

"But Rafferty, he took my arm, twisted it even. Said I had to go. Had to get my things and go. Said, 'Master Turner passed you on.'

"Made it sound like I wasn't nothing more than one of the shirts I sewed for his daughters, passed on to some smaller cousin. Passed on. It'd been better if he'd a killed me, than pack me off in a wagon and drag me away from my babies.

"'But I got's to say good-bye,' I says.

"But he say no.

"Didn't do no good to cry or pull back or let my legs go out from under me, he just dragged me to that wagon, and threw me in like a sack of cotton.

"Had me tied down and gagged at the mouth by the time I turned to check the fields for my boys. For my man Earl. All I could see in the rising light were the backs bent over hoes for row after row. I stared into that field until my eyes went to blurring, hoping for that one last chance to remember my babies. My Isaac, my Jacob. My Abraham.

"All I can remember is just gray eyes, a broken tooth, and the smell of hickory. That don't even amount to one boy and I had me three."

For Miss Rosie to be repeating that story, word must've reached her about Hattie. I kept to the wall, pressing into the wood, letting the splinters of it dig into me. With Mr. Caleb still gone, Hendersen might say Hattie's an orphan on account of the laws saying a child needs a father to be legal. Them laws ain't nothing but lies and wrongdoing. Like that Turner done to Miss Rosie by selling her away from her babies. Seeing her pain just tore me up inside like I done swallowed a bucket of nails.

Don't cry. Don't you cry, Stella Reid.

"Says she ain't ours," Miss Rosie said, doing the crying for me. "Says our Hattie ain't ours."

Miss Rosie brought Hattie into this here world. How they going to claim Hattie ain't Miss Rosie's?

"He say we not married. So she cain't be ours legal-like."

They sure enough were married. Old Agnes, she tell the story of they wedding each time the date come around again. I've been there for the telling, brought my own dish to pass to mark the occasion.

"He say I got to call Caleb home and we need us a marriage certificate." Miss Rosie stood up and started to pace, marking the end of her sadness and the beginning of her anger. "Hattie sent word of all they done and all that Hendersen said. They come take the wedding paper we got from that ceremony them Yankee soldiers done for us last year. Did it real slylike while she was gone. Them dogs."

"I never had me no certificate say I married my man Earl. But the Lord knowed we's married and he blessed us with those three fine babies. And when that deadhearted Turner done gambled me away like so much cash money and took my family from me, the Lord done give my heart to Caleb so's we could be married and have our Hattie child. Now that Mr. Hendersen say we ain't married and Caleb gone, so she ain't ours. He's made her some ward or something. Says he's responsible for her till she an adult 'lessen we can prove she's ours."

Miss Rosie turned to face me, giving me the look of death. "How we supposed to do that? He going to take the word of Miss Agnes who talked me through the birthing? I'll tell him every scar my Hattie got on her body! But that don't prove him nothing."

Something peculiar happened to me as I listened to her. I opened my mouth to speak and nothing came out. Not a single word popped into my head. Now, that'd never happened before. Silence and I are more familiar with each other than a fish is with water, but that's on account of me not saying what I'm thinking. I'd never come across a time when I couldn't think of something to say.

Miss Rosie took a deep, shuddering breath. "Hendersen won't even let her come home till we sign a paper says we'll work on his place until Hattie grown and we all free to go."

"Gabe come tell me, they got her living up in the young fellas' bunkhouse. All them took to the road like most of the folks around here, but not us. No, he got us by the heart." She grabbed her dress front and pulled. She bit back more words, then bowed her head to say a prayer—the sure sign she meant to cuss, but begged the Lord's forgiveness instead.

Wasn't her who needed to be begging the Lord. It was the likes of Lars Hendersen whose evil ways should have him on the very floor of the nearest church begging the Lord to get his burning soul out of hell.

"Mr. Quincy, he going up Natchez way for parts for the gin," I said. "He'll take word to Mr. Caleb. Call him home."

Miss Rosie nodded. "That'd be right fine, Miss Stella. And come morning, I'll go over to the Freedmen's Bureau, tell them what Hendersen done." Miss Rosie set to pacing again. "If'n they can prove Hendersen's paper ain't legal, we'd get us our Hattie back."

Miss Rosie sat down and set to rocking, folding her hands over her chest like she held a baby. She'd gone full around and soon she'd be chanting up her boys again. Couldn't watch it.

Had to leave, to stumble outside and fight with tears again. The natural water my mama's eyes could no longer make. How's a body go so dry it can't even shed tears no more. No sweat. No tears, just the jagged breath that says it's almost over.

Doctor tried to keep me out. Cousin Mertle's nurse Miss Katherine did too. Both of them got my teeth marks in their skin for their

23

trouble. I held my mama's hand when she left this here world. I said my good-byes. Didn't make her being gone any easier. Held my mind to the idea she'd gone home to Jesus, where every good soul belonged.

And a living soul like Hattie belonged with her mama and daddy, not in some bunkhouse the young field hands used before they took to the road headed north. I mounted that horse and rode hard to get home.

The idea of Hattie working cotton gave my hands the sting of boll cuts, the red, raw reminders of how tough a plant of cotton could be. I'd picked my weight in cotton a time or two, but not Hattie. No, that girl spent her days indoors, cleaning, dressing, and carting for the Hendersen girls.

Just like I didn't belong indoors with no dress or sissified nonsense like the stitching and music lessons Cousin Mertle's always tried to force on me, Hattie didn't belong in no field.

The riding had me bone jittery, but I asked Mr. Zachariah to put that horse up and made for Mr. Quincy's cabin so I could check in on Hattie before dawn caught me sneaking.

The door swung open before I knocked. Mr. Quincy must've seen me coming. "What you here to say, Stella Reid?" He looked down on me like he wished he could stomp me under his boot. "You got them papers your Daddy promised?"

Mr. Quincy done asked me that near about every time he saw me. Daddy promised he'd deed Oak Grove over to all the folks who worked it soon as he could find a lawyer to do the paperwork, but they ended Daddy's life before he could make good on his plan. Quincy knew it, but he still hated him for failing.

Made me feel like a dirty old bug to be standing there, but I came for Hattie and her kin. Not me. "Need to get a message to Mr. Caleb in Natchez."

"Do you, now?"

I could see Miss Isabella standing inside, hands holding her elbows, looking painful worried. Did she think Mr. Quincy'd put a hurt on me? Nawh. Anger had him riled, but not mean. Daddy'd made a powerful promise he couldn't keep. Mr. Quincy had something to be mad about.

"Hendersen's forcing Hattie to stay on."

"I know the feeling." Mr. Quincy stared down like he could drive me into the ground with his eyes. He felt tied to Oak Grove now that he didn't have no traveling money. Spent what he had on the bricks for the house he built for him and Isabella on the property that should've become theirs. Now the law said he didn't own the land or the house he built.

"Will you tell him?"

He grumbled his agreement then shut the door in my face.

With dawn rouging up the sky, I didn't have time to dwell on Mr. Quincy, so I headed down to the bunkhouse to find Hattie. Coming down the hill, I could see Old Baxter, Mr. Hendersen's overseer, sitting in the path with a shotgun in his lap. Didn't take him no time atall to stand up and put me in his sights.

"Should just blow you away, Stella Reid. Put me a wrong to right. White girl like you mixing with darkies ain't natural."

Times like that, I wanted to have the aim of David, just swing and bring that giant idiot to the ground, maybe knock some sense into his corn pone for brains.

Instead, I turned and walked off between the cabins, knowing he couldn't follow me. The darkness settling around the place would keep me hidden as I stepped into the trees. I made myself a little half circle, then came back with a sneak in my step to hustle under the bunkhouse. Crawled for the hatch the boys used to use to let themselves out at night and sneak over to Oak Grove so's they could make sweet on the girls they'd been courting.

"Stella, that you?" Hattie asked into the dark.

"Yep."

"Miss Stella Reid's in here?" asked another voice from the far side of the bunkhouse.

"Shush up," Hattie warned, but voices started chattering all around me like I was nothing more than a fox sneaking into the henhouse, so I stood up, then slammed that trapdoor down, letting those young'uns scream it out.

"Shut up in there or I'll come in and shut you up!" Baxter yelled.

Hattie grabbed me by the arm, then yanked me to her bunk. "What you doing in here?"

"Finding you." I figured the others I'd heard had to be the rest of the children Hattie had gone on about that morning.

"You got any of that chocolate you bring us last Christmas?" I knew that voice to be Miss Vera. That girl had her more than just a sweet tooth. She had a sweet mouth. She'd sell one of her own sisters for a lick at the sugar bowl.

"Go to bed, Vera," Hattie said.

Miss Vera, seventh daughter of Mr. Ben and his wife Miss Clara. Mr. Ben had given his life so his children could have freedom: Now look what Mr. Hendersen had done to them.

Thinking on them girls made me recall the first voice I'd heard. Dessa, Vera's older sister. Girl had a fascination with me. Kept rubbing my skin like she expected it to come off. But I suppose I had to be the only white person she was allowed to touch. And I bet the other five sisters were kept up in there somewhere. All of them under guard like runaways brought back.

"Why you come here, Stella? You can't do nothing."

Ain't nobody been too successful at telling me what I can and can't do since I first drew breath, but I didn't need to remind Hattie of that.

"This ain't going to do no good, Stella. I can't see you in this dark. How am I going to tell what you're saying to me if I can't see your face?"

"I saw your mama. She's at Potter's Creek. Coming home by morning light. Sent word to Mr. Caleb by way of Mr. Quincy. They'll sort this all out."

"You did!" She squeezed me so hard, she'd about wrung the blood out of my veins.

"Well, your word got to Miss Rosie first." Couldn't let her think she didn't have the biggest hand in setting the wheels in motion.

"Well, I won't be signing nothing till my papa gets here."

Heard Dessa grumble from not a foot away. "Least you got a papa to come."

Silence answered, but even in the faint light that had started to grow, I could see those two girls holding hands, saying *I'm sorry* through their palms.

Wished I could do more to help them girls. But I couldn't bring Mr. Ben back.

Hattie looked at me. "So, what you going to do, Stella? Heard about Oak Grove going up for auction."

With all of Hattie's troubles, I'd plumb forgot. No wonder Mr. Quincy had me pegged for dirt. He'd heard about the auction.

"We'll fix on a plan. Mr. Vinson'll call a meeting." The foreman, Mr. Vinson, would no doubt call a meeting before folks went to the fields—a meeting I had better get to if I wanted to be part of the solution.

"What sort of plan? You can't bid on that place of yours." Hattie huffed. "You'll have about as much luck finding you some money as you would keeping one of them chocolates Vera's been going on about from melting in the sun."

"She got some?" Vera piped up.

"No," Hattie snapped.

But Hattie had me thinking on the money Daddy kept stashed away for when we needed it. With Mama gone now and no will to say I had a claim on Oak Grove, we had us a right powerful need for that money. But could I find enough? I had to figure out just how much we needed, so I made for the door to head to meeting with the folks. Still, I worried after Hattie, so I said, "Send word what the bureau tells Miss Rosie."

As I slipped out the door, I heard Hattie asking above me, "You leaving?" But I was already crawling my way to the moonlight, so I could hightail it home for the meeting.

Going to Meeting

Heard the bell calling the meeting as I ran past the stables. Most days, moonrise called everyone on Oak Grove to meeting even though the laws in these parts forbade it. Like I said, things worked different on Oak Grove.

But them laws never did make any sense to me. Just goes to show most white men don't believe in nothing but their own rights. They fought them a war back in the colony days for what they called "inalienable" rights. That means you can't deny them. Can't withhold them. Yet those same fellas denied colored folks their rights. Even made up laws to take more away. One of them laws those colony boys fought for was the right to gather in peace. General Washington led their army straight through to Yorktown so's people could gather when they wanted, where they wanted. Then those soul-thin fools turned right around and said no colored folks could do the very same thing on account of them being black and from Africa.

But men like my father, who are true to the soul God gave them, know it don't matter where you're born or how long the sun touched your skin, you still have the rights God done handed down to you. No wonder the people who first called this land home used to say white men had forked tongues. Those people who floated on over from Europe like they owned the place could scream for rights out of one side of their mouths, then deny them out of the other side. Calling their tongues forked is an insult to snakes. White folks with such evil ways seemed more like two-headed demons to me.

Makes it so's a body trying to do the right thing has to do it in secret, like my daddy. Born a man who said what he believed and believed what he said, Daddy would always say, "The laws of man ought to see no color." Daddy never did. And he taught me to see the same way.

Once the moon hung itself over the old crooning tree, Daddy strode down to the meeting hall at the far end of the quarters to join in on the meeting, his vote counting like any other man or woman in the room. That's right, on Oak Grove, we even let the women vote. If they had to work, they had a vote. Mrs. Wynston started the vote on that rule. Mama was one of the first to support her—the only meeting Mama ever attended until Daddy died.

This morning's meeting started like its nighttime kin—with talk. Most nights, they spoke on who's with child. How things might be growing. Who took sick the night before. Just a time for folks who didn't see each other regular to set the record straight.

But that morning, fear had words sparking with "What we gonna do?" and all sorts of who-said-what and how's-that-going-to-change-things.

Then Pastor Rallsom called everyone to their chairs for a prayer—a good thanks for what they had and a kind request for what they didn't. That's when folks sat down—wife to husband, brother to brother, sister to sister—they all sat familylike around the edge of the room. Most folks left they walkabout babies to home with the older children, but Daddy used to bring me. Mama stayed to home, so I guess that made it okay for someone else from our family to show up. But I kept my lips shut tight, knowing I didn't have the age or the work behind me to have a say. In that chair beside my daddy, I'd watched Oak Grove change over the years, learned all the do and say of keeping a plantation on the grow. But in all those years, I never said a single word at meeting.

So, it seemed right peculiar to be sitting in Daddy's old chair, looking out at the folks lifting their heads out of prayer, waiting on Mr. Vinson to start the meeting.

But then Mr. Lennox, a tall man from Mr. Quincy's field crew, shouted, "Ain't there no Reids who keep their word?"

"Yeah!" Came a shout from behind him.

Folks started making a ruckus, some cheering Mr. Lennox, others shushing him.

Mr. Vinson stood up, holding his hands in the air, saying, "Now, Mr. Lennox. This is not how we do our business."

Mr. Lennox got to his feet. "Well, I know how them Reids do business. They don't pay their bills. So now we have to."

"Now you wait, Andrew Lennox," said Mr. Zachariah, waving the riding crop he used to keep the horses in line. "This meeting ain't started yet."

All that yelling and them questions flying had me knotted up inside. Near about felt hog-tied and ready to be thrown in a pot for boiling. So only a word came out when I tried to defend my Daddy. "Bullet."

All the fuss just swallowed that word right up, so I stood up and shouted it. "Bullet!"

"What?" Mr. Lennox turned to stare at me. His eyes pulled others to look in my direction. "What you say?"

"A bullet kept my daddy from keeping his promise. Now a lie's what's putting this place up for auction."

My words just sucked all the others out of the room. Folks knew my daddy died in front of the stables just down the way, shot in the back like a fella running from a fight. But my daddy didn't run from nothing. The real coward had to be the man with the gun who didn't even have the guts to let my daddy look him in the eye.

Stepping in front of Mr. Lennox, Mr. Quincy asked, "What kind of a lie?"

"Kind that says my daddy didn't pay his bills when he did."

"Well, if they say he didn't pay them, why didn't you?" asked Mr. Lennox, but I could hear a woman's voice say, "No woman child be paying no bills. Gots to be with her kin."

Felt those words trying to sweep me out the door like some critter that got into their house. But I had to stand my ground, defend my daddy and fight for what he wanted done. "Weren't no bill to pay till Richardson sent me them foreclosure papers."

"And now," Mr. Vinson shouted real loud to let folks know he had his own things to say, "we've got to decide what to do."

"To do?" barked Mr. Taylor Winfield from his chair in the corner. Shaking his head, he pulled on his gray beard. "Ain't nothing to do but see who's buying and what they gonna offer us."

A round of "that's right" answered him while others cursed the idea.

"Won't be working for no Richardson," Miss Katie yelled. "Man's the devil."

Mrs. Bishop crossed her arms and clucked her tongue. "Don't you go giving that sinner any room in here." And she wasn't talking about Richardson.

"Who says Richardson going to be the one owning this place?" asked Mr. Zachariah, just a-turning that crop over in his hand.

Sitting as still and as certain as a stone in the rapids, Mrs. Wynston said, "Ain't no guesswork to know who the top bidder going to be."

Owning the only hotel in town meant Richardson had the power to say who goes and who stays in Helensburg, but having the largest plantation in the state meant he had the banker, Mr. Markham, kowtowing like a house servant. After all, half the money in that bank in town belonged to Richardson. If he wanted the bank to take a property like Oak Grove, then Markham took it. Even if he had to lie to do it.

Done took Oak Grove claiming Daddy hadn't paid off the last of what he owed for the 120 acres he bought and paid for the winter before he died. Markham talked about overdue interest; I say that banker done evil that was overdue for punishment, but such things are the Lord's job.

And if I had the Lord's ideas straight in my head, my job happened to be seeing that Oak Grove went to the folks who really owned the place. And everyone in that room had pretty much the same idea in mind. Just had no way to make it happen.

Mr. Vinson said real loud, "Ain't nobody here wanting to work under Richardson, so we's got to get our minds set on this here thing."

"Set on what?" asked Mr. Quincy, pulling down that old hat

he never took off. "You thinking on buying the place at auction? Why don't you talk to Beeman about a black man showing his money around here? Look what happened to him when he tried buy himself a blacksmith shop."

Growing up going to meeting, I'd had myself convinced I knew the in and the out of everything on Oak Grove, but this news about our late blacksmith, Mr. Beeman, had me spinning in my drawers. He died the same night they killed my daddy. Tried to make it look like Mr. Beeman had him a stroke, but we found out he'd been struck dead in the head. Folks thought they'd done it to keep him out of the way when they shot Daddy. But, if they killed Mr. Beeman for trying to buy property in town, then they for sure killed Daddy for trying to turn Oak Grove over to the folks who worked it.

Mr. Jasper pulled my mind back to the meeting when he drummed his cane down to pop up out of his chair and shout, "I got me ten dollars!"

"Me and Zachariah have us five," said Maggie, our school teacher, trying to hush her child. All the racket had that baby just a-bawling.

"Seventeen. I can pay in seventeen."

"Twenty-one."

"Four and two bits."

Sounded like the auction'd already started, with folks calling out how much they could chip in.

Then Quincy stood himself up and bellowed as loud as a church bell, "Who got thirty thousand dollars?"

Folks froze up like someone said the ginning house had burned to the ground.

Knowing he had all eyes on him, Quincy lifted his chin and said, "That's how much we be needing. Land prices might be down, but they's still at ten or twelve dollar for an acre of good cotton land. And you know this place giving up more cotton than God's got rain. Not to mention that house out there is as big and sturdy as a king's. And you think they going to be giving us that gin, them stables, that blacksmith shop, and all of that? Place won't be selling for less than thirty thousand. We got that?"

You could see he'd taken a piece of soul out of every chest in the room. Folks dropped back into their chairs or took to sighing or staring off. They knew pooling all their money wouldn't add up to no ten thousand, let alone three times that.

Looking all hunched up, Mr. Jasper asked, "Can we buy us a piece with what we got?"

Folks gave the idea a few half-hearted "yeah"s.

But Mr. Lennox laughed all disgustedlike, saying, "You thinking they gonna let any of us bid?" He looked around the room. "You all remember what happened when Old Man Franklin willed him a piece of land to that woman he kept over at his place, so's their children could work it?"

Murmuring moved through the room like a rumor down the row. Everyone knew the white planter Franklin'd had him a mistress in the slave quarters, brought him five children into this world by her. None by his wedded wife. When he died, he left his wife the whole plantation and his mistress a small piece of land weren't even attached, but some low-water place a farmer'd have to fill in to make a seed grow. They burned that poor woman out, the smoke killing her youngest and the flames taking her house. Franklin's widow done said she'd do it again till all those children died.

That kind of hate made my soul ache.

Mr. Lennox asked, "You think they'll be selling us land?"

"We won this war, Andrew." Mr. Henry stood up, still wearing the pants the Union army done give him. "We got us the right to land. Here or anywhere in this country."

"That's right!" Mr. Zachariah shouted, sending up a chorus of "Yes, sir."

Mr. Quincy nodded. "We bid separate or together?"

"Together," Mr. Vinson said, sending up a round of affirmations. "They going to sell the fallow land first. Ain't no buyer going to want that land. Won't want to pay taxes on it. That's what we'll bid on."

"Now that's the best plan I heard yet!" Mr. Taylor stomped his foot.

Mrs. Wynston said, "Let's vote!"

And as the vote came in all "yea"s, I set to thinking, if the folks of Oak Grove bought that fallow land, it'd sit in Mr. Richardson's craw, cutting away at him like a piece of glass, and he'd do any old thing to get that glass out, including kill. For I knew like the sins of my own heart, that man killed my daddy.

Wasn't about to go against the plan they'd laid out, but I seen death hanging over it like a big old storm cloud. That meant I needed a plan of my own. Something to keep Oak Grove out of Richardson's hands all together. Daddy might've stored him some money around the place, but he sure didn't leave behind no thirty thousand dollars.

I needed me a plan. Some way I could get a legal hold on the place.

Set to praying, asking the Lord to put me on the right path.

As I watched the folks celebrating and talking and figuring on how much they had saved up to give, I thought the Lord gave me a sign by them blue Union pants on Mr. Henry and Mr. Lennox, and they were just two of the men who'd fought for freedom, then come home to family.

Yankees. That's who bought up land at these here auctions. Coming in with all their fancy ideas and Union money, buying up land to try their hand at planting. One of them Yankees might take a liking to some extra cash money. That's right. I'd find me a Yankee, then use Daddy's money to push the bid right out of Richardson's reach. Why, the Lord had a right nice idea there.

Maybe that Yankee'd give me a bit of stake in the place. A roof over my head. Not what I'd had in mind when the Good Lord told me I'd stay on, but I've learned what a body sees and what God means in a promise are rarely the same thing. Still felt right good to have me a plan.

Mr. Vinson sat next to me, his brow knitted. "Miss Stella."

I could see the worry working itself into the furrows of his brow. "Richardson going to want you to move into town now." He lowered his hand like he meant to put it on my knee, then pulled it back.

Mr. Vinson been voted in as foreman for each of the thirteen years since Daddy took the place over and he done a fine job of it too. We've seen more cotton go through our gin in that time than the sky's got clouds. Weren't two men on the place who spent more time together than him and my daddy, talking up plans, fixing things, building, doing what needed to be done. If Daddy put an idea up for the vote, Vinson came in to second. Daddy did the same for him.

Since Daddy died, Vinson ran the place, keeping Mama

informed, but she weren't one for planting, except in her own garden. Now he probably felt he had to see me off safe—a last favor to Daddy, I guess.

"I'll stay to Oak Grove."

"You planning on living in the trees?"

I smiled, wishing I could live on in Daddy's office like I had been, but I'd probably have to move on to maybe the cabin out past the stables where Daddy put up traders come to do business. "I'll find me a bed."

"Richardson ain't going to let you stay on, Stella. And I wouldn't want you near the man."

Funny, I felt the same way about Richardson being close to everyone else on Oak Grove. "He won't be here."

I stood up to leave.

"Now, Stella." Mr. Vinson started to follow me, but got pulled into a plan on how to collect and record money by Mrs. Wynston and Mr. Henry.

And I just sort of drifted out of there, feeling as pulled as cotton carded down to thread. Wasn't quite sure where the wind of God would blow me next.

Money, Blood or Otherwise

Daddy had him a good deal of money hidden away, but not the likes of what we needed to keep Oak Grove. As I walked an idea sort of followed me. That money had roots in slavery. And there weren't nothing I could do to pull them roots up. Fought hard to clean my soul of the idea that no matter how good my daddy had been to the folks, he'd still owned human beings like cattle. Not that he ever wanted such a thing. Inherited most of that ownership from his daddy. What folks he "bought" he did so to bring family to family. And once they's reunited, he'd write them freedom papers, give them a choice to stay on or head north. Most folks choose to stay on because heading north from Oak Grove meant slipping out from under the watchful eyes of the planters in these parts who sought to put a noose around the place and choke us all dead for trying to go against their ways.

On account of that, Daddy moved real slow, writing papers and keeping them safe, then sending folks north real secretlike when he could. By the time the war broke out, weren't no one on the place who needed to be "freed" by the Union Army. Why, weren't a body there who couldn't come and go as they pleased.

Not that we let that little fact be known to anyone off the place.

Still, the idea that Daddy ever had him ownership over a living, breathing soul had me cold in a way no amount of quilts could warm up. And I tried. Believe me. Pulled one over me like a shawl to search up Daddy's office for the money.

Since the day they carried my mama out the back door in a box, I hadn't set foot in the house my great-granddaddy had built. Never did seem like my house anyhow. Just a big old empty building full of fancy curtains, shiny as a mirror furniture, and beds big enough for a horse. No, I liked Daddy's office just fine. I'd slept down there many a night when Daddy stayed up to settle the books or plan things out.

And I cursed myself for not paying more mind when Daddy put money or papers in his big-as-a-boulder safe. Now it just sat there looking all shiny and proper. And I would've bet my own toes that's just where Daddy had put them papers we needed to prove he meant to turn Oak Grove over to the folks who worked it. But I couldn't get that dag-blasted safe open!

I'd tried every darn thing I could think of. Daddy's birthday. Mama's birthday. My birthday. The day they got married. Every time I walked by that safe, I tried another combination, but didn't a one of them work.

Lucky for me and the folks, Daddy never believed in keeping his money all in one place, so I set to collecting. I'd seen Daddy dip in for a few bills to buy a new harness, pay for a doctor when one of the folks fell sick, and even buy a fine new dress for Mama on her birthday.

Most folks took to burying their money come the war, knowing Yankees searched for gold and bills, anything they could use to buy what they didn't steal from plantations. But Oak Grove never saw the Yankees come a-stealing. They always sent an officer who stopped at our front gate, called out as kind as a man looking to buy a horse, "Mrs. Reid, can you spare some food for a few hungry men?"

That led to a picnic of sorts down by the creek, men gobbling down whatever Mrs. Wynston brought out there. Mama always slipped a few bills in with the tablecloths she sent along, knowing the money and food might keep the soldiers from coming back to steal what they needed. And it did for the entire war.

That sure wasn't the tale for most places around Helensburg, but then most planters didn't send money to the Union army like my daddy did—about as regular as he hid money in the bottom of the windowsill in his office, under the floorboards below his desk, in the casement of the hay loft door in the barn, behind the loose bricks in the well house—in every little place he could think to hide it. Hidden from his own daddy when he first started to raise the money to buy family back, then from Mama who wanted him to account for things regular, then from them ragtag Confederate militia men coming in looking for donations. Daddy gave them a bill or two to keep them from fining him, but he never did let a soul know just how much he had at the place.

Spent the whole day hunting up all the money I could find. Turned out he'd stowed away nearly one thousand dollars. Made me wonder if I shouldn't just pitch in with the rest of the folks. That'd buy about one hundred acres, I thought, sitting there on the floor of the stables with that money in my lap. But still, a hundred acres wasn't hardly enough for more than a few families to raise cotton, let alone all seventy or so folks left at Oak Grove.

They'd still have to raise enough for the other eighteen hundred and fifty acres on the place.

Staring out the stable door, I could almost see Daddy walking out to lean on the casing and have a look-see at the moon. I'd have walked up to him, leaned on his hip, so he could put his arm on my shoulder and tell me how they think that moon's nothing more than a big old rock caught in the pull of the earth.

"Kind of like this!" he'd say, grabbing my arms and swinging me around as he spun a tight circle in the dirt. Faster and faster we'd go until he let my hands free and I went flying, landing in the hay in the yard.

"My heavens, the moon done got away," he'd say and we'd laugh.

If Mr. Beeman, our blacksmith, had him a pay-by-the-piece job he'd been working on after supper, he'd come out and chat with us, his face still glowing with sweat in the moonlight.

I could almost see him standing there, smiling out at us, hear the jingle of the keys he kept hanging off the tail ends of his leather apron. I loved those keys as a knee-hugging child. Always tried to catch them when he walked to the blacksmith shop in the morning.

At the door, he'd shake them keys at me, then turn around and say, "Now chile, get on home to your mama. I got me some work to do. This ain't no safe place for no chile."

Wasn't no safe place for him neither. They killed him there. The doc Mama brought in said they brained him with his own tongs. I buried them with him—my way of giving back at least a piece of what they took from him. After all, Mr. Beeman had used those tongs to work the trade that would buy his family home.

When he died, I figured they'd killed him for trying to save Daddy by warning him or something. But Mr. Lennox said he died for trying to buy a blacksmith shop in town. Never even thought on his savings till Mr. Lennox spoke on it. What I didn't understand now was why they'd kill a man just for wanting his own shop. Why, he'd done work for half the people in Helensburg one time or another. Them nearsighted fools just couldn't see their way clear of allowing a black man to own a business in town. And what kind of evil is it that they'd kill to keep things as they saw them? Made it mean all the more to me that I did what I could to help protect Oak Grove, prevent more men from dying like Mr. Beeman did.

Standing in the shop, I touched the hood over the pit to get a feel for that soot I knew so well. Loved that blackened-bacon smell of burned wood. Felt the heat of the fire in my memory as I watched old Mr. Beeman turning a red-hot horseshoe over the fire. I'd come to him to ask for a box where I could lock away my money and keep it safe after Ginny Matheson done stole the coins I kept for buying marbles, saying they fell out of my pocket.

Mr. Beeman, he looked at me, his face shiny black with sweat and soot. "You know the safest place for your money, chile?"

I waited.

"Bury it where's folks are too afraid to find it."

Now, that made good sense. I headed straight for Mama's beehives and buried it under there. Them bees never stung me on account of the fact I didn't fear them or move too quick. I just dug me a hole and put my jar of coins in the ground. Ginny Matheson'd never go there.

Standing over that pit, looking down at the coals that still smoked from the day's heat, I realized Mr. Beeman had given me another grab at his keys. But this key hid inside that secret he shared with me.

"Bury it where's folks are too afraid to find it."

With a fire hot enough to melt the head of an ax, only a fool wouldn't fear a blacksmith's pit. I got me a hook and opened the door below, didn't see nothing but ash. Grabbed a shovel and started pitching the coals into buckets. With the pit coal free, I started tapping around with the shovel. The hollow of the oven below rang back, then *ting, ting,* I hit something solid on the back edge. Putting on the leather gloves and using the hook, I fished around for a door, something to tell me what he'd put under there. Sure enough, I found a door. It took a lot of scraping and prying to get it open, but I didn't see nothing but black. Reaching in, I found a metal box. Heavy enough to be filled with bricks, I near about fell over trying to get it out. Practically dropped it to the floor.

Opened that thing up and found it to be metal on metal on metal, then lined with bricks, then wood, then another metal box that opened up to show me all the money Mr. Beeman had saved. No amount of heat could get through all that to touch his money. And he had himself a bank in there. Not a hundred dollars or two, had to be over a thousand dollars. He'd started saving years back so's he could buy home his son and grandsons.

I remember them days, how he'd count out the payment for each bill he collected, telling me, "They'll be coming soon, Miss Stella. Real soon." Tucking the money away under his apron, he'd step outside for a fresh breath of air, then say, "I'll be putting my boys one step closer to heaven by bringing them here to Oak Grove."

Turned out those boys brought their own selves here. When the Union crossed into Tennessee, his boy just up and walked his family out of there and straight to Oak Grove, giving Mr. Beeman the reunion his heart ached for. That freed him up to save for the shop he hadn't even allowed himself to dream about until his family saw freedom.

Sitting there, staring at that money, I couldn't help but see Mr. Beeman's blood on it. Tried to tell myself Mr. Beeman would've wanted his kinfolk to have all that he'd saved. But that didn't stop me from wanting to keep that money myself, use it to buy the rest of Oak Grove away from Richardson, keep that dandified demon from getting his hands on all my daddy had fought to keep. Felt the pull of it tearing at my heart.

But I had to do right by Mr. Beeman. He'd been loyal to my daddy, after all. Like Mr. Vinson, Mr. Beeman'd had his freedmen's papers for years, but he stayed with Daddy. "Never find me a fairer man in this here world," he told me one day.

And I had to be true to Mr. Beeman's memory and give that money over to Mr. Beeman's son, Garrett. I carried that money back to Daddy's office. Funny how it felt as heavy as if I'd kept it in that box Mr. Beeman had made. Knew deep down in my bones that it wasn't right keeping that money, but I had to hold on to it for a while, just enough time to give my mind a bit to give up on the idea before I let go of that money.

Putting Mr. Beeman's savings under the floor beneath the bed, I bundled up Daddy's money and put it in his going-to-town bag, then said a prayer over it.

Even had another go at that safe, hoping I just might crack it. Tried the date for the day Daddy took over Oak Grove, 12-21-53.

Day Granddaddy died. Three days after my first birthday. Turn the lock left to number 12. Past 21 going right and back to it, then left to 53. Pull. No give.

By then all my hope had turned cold. I layed down, knowing the money that killed Mr. Beeman rested right under me. And there weren't no thinking on Mr. Beeman's death without remembering Daddy lying there face up to the moon. I'd dropped down beside him, saying, "It's time to go to meeting, Daddy. Time to go to meeting." Like the duty of it might bring him back.

Don't know where my mind went a-walking that night. Just wanted my daddy to take my hand and lead me down the row to the meeting hall. But his hand had gone cold, my daddy leaving it behind for the body waiting on him in Heaven. I kissed that hand just as Mr. Vinson come and scooped me up to get me out of all the yelling and ruckus that started when folks realized someone done took my daddy from this world.

To pull my mind away from the sorrow that held it, I set to my log-writing duties. Since the days when Great-Grandaddy Hiram kept him a log on the plantings and growings of Oak Grove, every Reid done kept a log on the place. Daddy'd buy himself a fine book of smooth paper and leather binding. Did his building plans in there, kept track of the crops, the livestock, the orchard, every little thing that happened on the place, even drew him some maps.

As a scribbling child, I'd copied him, using scraps and a lead on the floor of his office. Now I kept that log for real. When I took over his last book, I'd imagined I'd only do an entry or two until Daddy came back, but it'd been over a year now and I had more entries in the thing than Daddy did. Just didn't seem right.

With the day's log done, I curled up in my bed, a prayer on my lips, and quilts up over my head. Didn't do me no good. Still felt wrong inside. Not just about that log, but about the whole place, how the folks just wanted to shuffle me off to town for fear of what I'd do against them. All those years they'd been working for my daddy didn't seem to mean a thing. Or it didn't mean enough compared to the idea that Daddy had laid a legal claim on their lives at one time. A claim they wanted to break once and for all.

Can't say I blamed a soul for that, but Daddy never wanted to make such claims from the start. What he wanted to see was a plantation run like a family, everyone working side by side for the same goal—"good cotton, good food, good times," he'd say, stuffing a napkin in his collar before digging in to the noon meal served out under the arbor.

But goodwill can't wash an evil like slavery away. And that fact had me all twisted up inside. So I just set to praying. I let my heart do the leading as I asked for a way into knowing what I could do to make good on Daddy's promise, a clear idea of how to get into that safe, a way to help Miss Rosie and Mr. Caleb to free poor Hattie, my mind just kept spinning through prayer after prayer like I'd set them up on a wheel.

All that wondering and praying left me kind of dizzy. But I went back to praying, begging for the Good Lord's guidance to know a way around the problem of keeping Oak Grove whole. Couldn't buy much more than a field of cotton with the money of Daddy's I'd found, but the Lord already done told me, Oak Grove would stay under my feet for the rest of my life and I'd always been inclined to take the Lord at His word.

What a Secret's Worth

Had glasses clinking in my head as Mrs. Wynston and her daughter Mary Ellen cleared dinner dishes before I realized I'd half-slept, half-worried my way into a memory. I could see a group of lady folk just a-whispering up a storm from my post beneath the buffet table, a whole row of desserts over my head like a funny kind of hat. This was not my idea of Liberty.

On Oak Grove, we called Saturdays "Liberty" on account of it being the day nobody worked. Sunday was the day we worked for the Lord. But Saturdays were all your own.

Now, on Liberty, we usually went upriver for some good country music with the folks Daddy been partnering with to bring in their cotton for a good price—folks who work their own fields and keep up with what it means to be Southern in Daddy's eyes: tend your land, raise your family, and fiddle your way to heaven. That was Daddy's idea of a good life. That's what put him in the field right alongside every other body working on Oak Grove. Daddy always said, "Don't ever ask a man to do what you wouldn't do yourself."

Well, the war pounded all that to dust. Most of them work-a-field farmers marched off to fight. Come nightfall my parents sat up in the parlor and talked while Daddy tried to read the paper without getting spitting mad and Mama tried to do her needlework without pulling it too tight—what with all of Daddy's carrying on about the war and such, he had her nerves tugged tighter than that thread. Least that's what I could see from my usual post under the table.

But not that night; the evening I recalled had a darker turn to it. Daddy had tried, once more, to keep a promise to Granddaddy about making friends among the planters to build alliances and such. Granddaddy said Daddy'd need those men on his side to get a fair price for his cotton and see it head upriver. Planters in these parts could make things evil hard on a fella who didn't play their little games. And being a man of his word, Daddy had tried to treat those planters right, but those old coots didn't have a civil bone in their bodies.

Never could understand why Daddy invited most of them dolled-up snobs into our house anyhow. Had to be another way to try and make nice with those fools. Then again, weren't a Southerner in the whole county that didn't warm up to a good party. That could be a surefire way to get those fellas to playing fair. But when Mrs. Wynston laid out the desserts, that little gathering turned ugly, thanks to that no-account Richardson.

"Makes them darkies so uppity, can't tell them what for!" he said from his post in the corner, a drink in his hand, his wife on his arm.

And like loyal little subjects of their crooked king, the men around him nodded and raised a glass, going on about this fella and that one, saying all kind of trash about the folks of Oak Grove.

"I'm surprised you don't just invite them in here," Richardson said, setting the people around him to laughing.

Daddy stood to have a word, but Mama stayed him with a hand over his wrist. I could see the anger dripping down the creases in Daddy's forehead, but he forced himself a smile, then said, "They've got an early morning of work ahead."

"So yours do some work for you then? I've been wondering if they don't just lie around and read," Mr. Ellis, the lawyer, chimed in, sending up another round of laughter. That fool could've eaten his glass and died for all I cared.

But Daddy kept his cool, pointing toward the quarters. "Isn't a man or woman down there who doesn't do the work of three."

"You breed them right, then, do you?" asked Hendersen from his chair at the euchre table.

Daddy looked about ready to break that table over the man's head and I sure wanted to help, but he said, "The folks of Oak Grove marry and have children by the blessing of God. I leave to God what's God's to have. How about you, Mr. Hendersen?"

"God gave the beasts of the field to man to manage, now, didn't He?"

Daddy near about cracked his own teeth, he clenched them so hard, but he said, "You know, I do wonder just what the Good Lord has in store for the men who take it upon themselves to make the Word of God fit their own twisted ideas." Daddy crossed the room to stand over Hendersen. That old fool didn't look so sure of himself now that he stared up at Daddy, who asked, "Suppose you could send me a message from the Good Lord Himself after you pass on? Or do you think you'll be a bit too busy fighting fires?"

That bloated old planter, Mr. Hendersen, stood up, snapping his chair to the wall with a flick of his knees. "Now, see here!"

"Oh, now, Lars, don't you let this Yankee-lover have at you like that." Richardson came over, smoothing out Hendersen's coat and acting all soothing. "He knows we only come here to entertain ourselves with his back-to-front ideas. It's like watching a monkey do tricks."

Laughter.

I had a mind to pick up a few plates and start throwing.

Mama stood at the door. She opened it and said, "Mr. Richardson, would you be so kind as to show me a trick and disappear?"

Richardson just smirked, then said, "You know, Miss Gayle Anne, it's so sweet how you try to live up to your Southern upbringing, but such a shame how far you fall from the mark. Your mama must be grateful for the grave she's in so she doesn't have to see her daughter so low."

Daddy swept in behind Richardson, grabbed him by the back of the collar with one hand, then pulled his arm up behind him with the other and scooted him right out the door like some stray dog that got in.

Richardson let out a hoot and a holler. Folks started shouting and carrying on. That place emptied out like someone'd shouted, "Hurricane!"

Mama stood at the door laughing. Daddy leaned against it, shaking his head.

"Never again."

"You think he'd come back?" Mama bit back a laugh.

"Not hardly." Daddy headed for the stairs. "And good riddance."

"So much for honoring your father's wishes." Mama followed him.

"Big Daddy only said I had to *try* to keep up his old alliances. Don't think he really expected me to do it, do you?" Daddy stopped at the top of the stairs.

"He never was a man to believe in miracles," Mama said, undoing Daddy's tie.

Daddy laughed, then turned toward their bedroom, calling down, "Stella, you ready for bed now?"

I stepped out.

"Stella!" Mama jumped. She knew not to wait for me to speak, so she asked, "How long have you been down there?"

Daddy looked at her like she'd asked how often cows come in for milking. "She's been there since dinner started."

"She has?"

I headed up after them.

"Yes, ma'am." Daddy walked off and just like that, what had been a talk on how silly it was to even entertain the likes of Richardson turned into a full-blown fight between Mama and Daddy.

Mama already had her bees a-humming when she told me to go to my room. I stepped inside, but then out my window onto the roof of the porch, so I could climb onto the veranda. I hightailed it to my favorite hiding spot, under the table outside their bedroom, to wait for those bees to come flying out. Mama always muttered under her breath when anger got a hold on her and set off a mess of them little critters in her mouth. Sounded just like the bees she kept down by the creek.

Mama kept her hive going until she felt good and ready to have her say, then plug your ears 'cause the yelling's gonna start. Stomping into their bedroom, Mama pulled off her earrings and threw them on the dressing table, then let the words fly. "It's one thing for a grown man to make his own path, but you can't let a young girl just have her way like that. It's not natural."

I knew Mama didn't take kindly to my spying, but it just felt so natural good to be out under that table on their veranda, the tablecloth like a shawl over me, but just lacy enough to afford me a nice view.

Mama started to comb out her hair, but she looked mad enough to pull it straight out of her head. Daddy came up behind her and rubbed her shoulders to calm her down and work that ugly look of fear out of her face. "She's too natural, if you ask me. Never paying any mind to the rules of this here world. What I wouldn't give for that kind of freedom."

"Freedom, Sebastian? You call that freedom? I call it a curse. Won't find a man in this state who'll take her for a wife. Just what will she have then?"

Daddy kissed her head. "Oak Grove, if I have my way." He winked at me as I waved from under the table.

Mama looked into the mirror. The sadness in her eyes made me weak in the heart. I had to turn away.

She whispered to Daddy. "Folks are saying she's sick, Sebastian."

Mama spoke true. Folks had been speaking on my odd ways since I could remember, saying my parents had been burdened with a touched child. Some even said I came out so sinful and peculiar that I'd spoiled Mama's womb from receiving any more seed and that's why she never did have any more babies after me. Made me feel dirty and wrong, but those twisted-up feelings never went away when I tried to act regular—keeping my sidewinding ideas to myself, wearing dresses, saying my pleases and my thank yous, and keeping myself occupied in ladylike ways that made my fingers sore and my tummy sour. I never wanted to be no burden, but I didn't want to pretend to be somebody I wasn't, neither.

But Daddy understood. He said, "It's just her way, Gayle Anne. It's just her way." He sat on the bench beside Mama to take her hand.

"Her way is going to get her locked up." Mama pulled her hand back.

"They've been saying the same thing about me for years." Daddy pulled off his favorite boots. I could see the shining stars in the soles just a-blinking at me.

"No, they've been saying your ways will get you killed. And I believe them." Mama stared at him in her mirror. Daddy looked back at her, his eyes as still and deep as hers. But his held a strength that said, *I'll do what's right, even if kills me.*

Hers saying back, *That's just what I'm afraid of.*

And they both spoke true. Daddy died for what he believed. Took a bullet to the heart 'cause he wouldn't give in to the likes of Richardson. Even before the Yankees came knocking, talk of Daddy being a sympathizer and a "darkie lover" started turning ugly. Such a name makes my blood boil. How dare they speak of fellow people of God with such mean and dirty words. In my way of thinking, saying such things would turn God Himself against them. And all that talk didn't stop Daddy from sending money to the Union army or letting colored folks know where they might find troops to take them in and get them to freedom. He gave that kind of know-how to our folks and other folks traveling north. And that's probably what got him killed.

But like most secrets in these parts, even those who knew them lied about what they knew. Richardson teased Daddy about his sympathizing in public, asking him how long his money had been turning blue. Or, did he think he'd be able to bring a crop in this year with so few hands tending the fields.

"You got yourself a sickness over there to your place, Reid? Or just what's happened to all your darkies down there in the hollow?" Richardson asked from his seat on the balcony of the hotel he owned.

That sent up a round a laughter among balcony-sitters and board-walkers alike.

Daddy didn't even look up, just lifted me into the wagon, then got in and flicked the reins to set the horses to walking. And I watched their tails twitch as we rode off with Richardson yelling this and that. Daddy stayed stiff backed and straight faced. I tried to follow suit, but I felt that yelling deep in my gut, twisting and turning, telling me things had turned sour for us.

The worry of it had me up nights, sitting on the roof outside my bedroom window, praying no harm would come. But come it did, in a gunshot that nearly sent me flying off that roof. Showed me just how fast I could slide down and jump to the ground. I ran until my lungs came up short of air.

But too much ground stood between me and the stables. I didn't make it there before Daddy's soul left his body. Left his eyes empty. His skin sickness white. His blood like a wicked halo around his head and shoulders. I held his hand, staring and panting, praying I'd fallen into a nightmare that'd end when Mama shook me awake.

But it was Mr. Vinson who shook me into letting go of Daddy's hand. He scooped me up and ran back to the house with me. Didn't have no grip on the here and now to fight him. Just let him run me through the screaming and the yelling and the running of all the folks trying to make heads or tails of the situation.

Can't recall much after that. Mama wailing. Someone shouting about Mr. Beeman. "No, it can't be," they said. But it was. Daddy'd been shot dead just feet from the stable door. And they found Mr. Beeman in his shop, eyes wide open, body twisted like he'd had himself a stroke.

Mama told me later that men came to sort things out—more like to set their lies in stone. Did them a head count. Mr. Chance came up missing, so they blamed the deaths on him. Said he and Daddy fought over Mr. Chance leaving.

"Everyone knows Reid couldn't lose another worker like that Mr. Chance. Works like a bull, that boy." Mr. Caleb told me that's what Richardson said, all proud. Mr. Chance had been born on the Richardson's place. And Richardson never did like Daddy having any of his "slaves," as he called them. But Daddy done bought Mr. Chance free and clear when Richardson had some money trouble. So Mr. Chance was free to come and go.

Daddy would have never tried to stop him. He knew Richardson had sold Mr. Chance's wife and son before him. Daddy even tried to help Mr. Chance find his family. He would have done what he could to help if Mr. Chance ever wanted to leave, but he'd stayed 'cause he figured his family would find him come freedom time.

But they never did 'cause Richardson and his lot hunted poor Mr. Chance down and killed him. Hanged him from a tree and left him there for days—a reminder of who still had the upper hand.

The Upper Hand

Riding into his hotel as he always did at dawn, Richardson sang out from the road the next morning all gloat and ugliness, "Twelve more days to glory, hal-a-loo, hal-a-loo. Twelve more days to glory, hal-a-loo."

Quite the rooster he turned out to be. Daddy used to tell me, if they had a rooster that crowed too early in the morning, Granddaddy'd cook the thing for supper. I wished I could just ship mine off to a faraway jungle so deep it'd take him a lifetime to find his way out again.

But no, he had to be riding past our place at dawn, just a *cock-a-doodle-do*ing that made-up little song of his. Heard him laugh to himself as he kept riding. Prayed God might put a little rain down on his parade, but the Good Lord decided in favor of the cotton and kept it nice and dry. We'd had too much rain that spring. The cotton needed time to grow and dry out by harvest time.

And I needed to get myself behind a hoe and start weeding. The work pulled the worries out of my head. Had folks talking on me. Didn't nobody find it regular for a white girl to be working the fields, but I did what I felt called to do.

Opened the door to find Hattie standing there, looking downright ready to eat a bear raw. "Hendersen say that contract legal since I got no papa to fend for me and my mama ain't got no job."

Hendersen done fired Miss Rosie? All so's he could claim she didn't have no money to care for Hattie. That fool had me mad enough to curse his soul.

Hattie followed me out to the field, yelling up her very own storm.

"And he ain't acting like Papa coming home is going to do us any better, saying he don't know Papa's my daddy what with my folks not being married and all."

As I fell in line with the folks already working and set to hoeing, Hattie kept her wind up and went right on yelling.

"He's not my daddy? Says who? That little devil on his shoulder that Mr. Hendersen answers to?" She spat on the ground. "I spit on that man. May his soul rot."

I figured it already had.

"And my folks got themselves married by that preacher over at Potter's Creek the summer they met, and that lieutenant over in the Yankee camp done a ceremony for them not even a year ago. Why, they been married more times than most. But that Hendersen, he done stole their certificate. I'm so mad I can't get my mind around nothing but devilment. What you think I should do?"

Mr. Jasper handed her a hoe. "I think you should work the ground like you working them gums of yours."

Now that put a smile on me.

"This ain't funny!" Hattie hit the hoe into the dirt. That girl

59

didn't even know how to hold a hoe, no wonder they kept her in the house to work. "What am I supposed to do? I can't work in that house no more. I'm ready to poison that old fool."

Sounded like a good plan to me. Even decided to help her with it. "Mrs. Wynston's got her a little root to cook. Put some on his grits. It'll keep him on the chamber pot."

"She got that?"

I nodded.

She dropped that hoe and ran off to the kitchen. Now, a little root wouldn't be solving her problems, but it'd be making her feel better while her daddy put his hand to finding that lieutenant who married them. Funny how a piece of paper's gotta say a couple like Miss Rosie and Mr. Caleb is married when the Good Lord done marry them nearly two decades ago through that preacher. But what white man's going to take the word of a black preacher. So much for their respect for the Word of God.

As I watched Hattie running off down the row, I couldn't help but see all them folks bent down with their hoes and think on Miss Rosie searching the fields for Isaac, Jacob, and her man Earl. Was she still married to Earl in her heart? In God's eyes? Daddy'd helped Miss Rosie try to find word of those boys and her man Earl for years, but hadn't heard word one.

With freedom and all those folks moving north and the bureau putting up notices and such, Miss Rosie'd have better luck. But she couldn't be searching now that Hendersen had his hands on Hattie. He'd say Miss Rosie'd given up her child.

I had to do something to help. Miss Rosie done said she'd been gambled off a place in Alabama down Mobile way. Said "gambled" on account of the fact that Old Mr. Turner done bet her in a poker game. Miss Rosie lost her family 'cause that man couldn't get the cards for no flush.

The very idea had me tearing up weeds faster than a hurricane could take down trees. Come the dinner bell, I headed straight for Daddy's office.

First, I tried the day Daddy paid the last bill on the land he'd bought from Hendersen to add another 120 acres to Oak Grove. Left to 6. Did I hear a click? Right past 17 and back to it. Left to 64. Pull.

Nothing.

Time to write. I wrote me a letter to the Freedmen's Bureau in Mobile, asking after those boys. Didn't know much, except about Isaac's gray eyes and Jacob's tooth, but I did know Miss Rosie and how she left Turner's plantation, so I described her up real good to post for her boys to find. They had to be looking for her. They know'd she'd been sold Natchez way, so I copied up that letter and that description for the bureaus in Hattiesburg, Biloxi, and McComb, any old place between here and Mobile where them boys might look.

A knock at the door sent me drawing a line of ink through my last letter.

"Miss Stella?" Heard old Mr. Jasper through the door.

Didn't answer, but that wasn't nothing peculiar.

"Just checking on you, Miss Stella. You ain't come back to work."

Howdy! I'd been writing so long the dinner hour done pass away.

I flew out that door and into the fields, leaving Mr. Jasper a-laughing at my door.

Just before the supper bell rung, Mr. Vinson stopped by. "Evening, Miss Stella."

"Mr. Vinson." I leaned on my hoe.

"Folks be wondering what you'll be doing next, Miss Stella." He looked at me kind of sideways, hinting that he had more on his mind than he planned on saying.

I waited. Didn't feel like talking until he showed me his cards. I guess you could say I planned on calling his bluff.

"You going into town to live with your cousin?"

Man knew me from my bottle-sucking days. How could he even think on me holed up with that poor old woman and all her rules about being a lady? I'd rather be right where I stood, hoe in hand, thank you very much. And Mr. Vinson knew that to be true.

He took in a big plug of air, then asked, "You fixing on bidding on the fallow land yourself?"

Glory be. The folks of Oak Grove thought I planned to try and buy the land away from them. How could they think that of me? Made me feel no bigger than the rocks under my feet, but I said, "Not the land you're bidding on."

He nodded toward the house. "You got you enough to bid on the place here?"

"If I did, you can be sure it'd go to all of you like Daddy planned."

"It would?" He raised his eyebrows.

"But I don't."

His shoulders slumped. Then he shook his head, kind of angrylike, saying, "Then just what do you have planned?"

"Keeping the rest of the place out of Richardson's hands, that's all."

He squinted at me all confused, then said, "Well, as long as you ain't planning on trying to outbid us."

With that, he just turned to leave, like business is business. I ran to catch him. "Mr. Vinson."

"Yeah."

I didn't even have words to put to the feelings that had my mind turning itself inside out. "You think I'd do you wrong?"

He closed his eyes a second. Then he looked at me to say, "Miss Stella, truth is every man I've known who's trusted a white man's promise has been left with less than nothing."

Mr. Beeman. Old Man Franklin's Mistress. Mr. Chance. The names just came tumbling into my head, all the people who'd seen death on account of dealings with white men who didn't keep their word or honor the words of others. Even my daddy couldn't keep his. He'd died trying, but he never kept it just the same.

The idea had my heart shrinking like a dead old piece of fruit drying in the sun.

"Then I won't make no promises."

"Miss Stella, you got to understand, you're just a young lady. Ain't nothing you can do here, but step aside and let the men do their business." He patted my shoulder, then walked off.

Felt like he'd just swept me off a porch like so much dirt. Didn't have no weight 'cause my kind don't keep their promises and I ain't old enough nor man enough to amount to much. Well, I never. Man done stood by my Daddy for all my life, but he walked right on over me.

Felt one of Daddy's rages building up—the kind of anger that sends you to screaming and throwing and breaking things, but I ain't my daddy. I ain't all the people who made promises and paid them in pain. No, sir. I'm Stella Reid. And I'm going to do right by my Daddy's promise no matter who believed I could.

A Sense of Ownership

At first light, I got up to take them letters I'd written to find Miss Rosie's boys to the bureau, but the idea didn't settle right, had a sharp kind of edge to it, telling me I'd come at it all wrong. Should've gone to Miss Rosie first, had her tell me what to say in them letters.

What a fool. Who else but Miss Rosie would know about her boys?

I rushed right over to Hattie's cabin, only to find Miss Rosie out back having her a battle with her garden, attacking them weeds like they's evil.

The way she smacked that hoe down, had me a little fretful to say how do.

But Miss Rosie seen me and stopped. Resting on that hoe, she said, "Morning, Miss Stella. Don't 'spose you've caught sight of my Caleb this morning?"

I shook my head.

She sighed. "Well, I'm sure the Lord's guiding his feet home." Set to hacking away again like she didn't quite believe her own words.

But they gave me an idea of how to tell her what I'd come to do. "Thinking on letters to do your walking."

She looked at me all confusedlike.

I held up one of the letters I'd written. "To find your boys."

Her hand shook as she took the letter I had all folded up and ready to send. "This about my boys?"

"Yes, ma'am."

"It's thick." She raised and lowered her hand like she weighed it, then passed it back to me. "You going to send those out to bureaus and such?"

"Yes, ma'am, but I don't have much more than what you said about them boys in here."

Staring off she said, "Don't know no more." Shaking her head, she set to striking at the ground again. "Can't write me no long letters. Can't leave to find them. Can't lay claim to my own child here at home." And *crack!* She brought that hoe down so hard she near about split a rock in two, sending it flying against a fence post.

She had me nailed to my spot, feeling all kinds of guilty for not being able to do more to help.

Then real suddenlike, she said, "Hold on to that tail"—an expression that always put a smile on my face. Then she put that hoe down and went inside real quicklike. Coming back, she had a paper of her own. "You get this in the *Christian Record*, it go out to all the black churches. They can announce it before the service."

I took the paper, recognized Hattie's writing straightaway, the words spelling out an advertisement looking for Miss Rosie's boys. "Seeking three sons born to a Miss Rosie, good at sewing, on

Turner Plantation, Mobile, Alabama. Sons named Isaac, Jacob, Abraham born to a father name of Earl, field hand. Miss Rosie sold up Natchez way twenty years ago, in the fall. Boys be twenty-nine, twenty-six, and twenty-one by now. Send word to Miss Rosie at the Hendersen Plantation in Helensburgh, Mississippi."

"Will do." I nodded, folding the paper up to put it in my pocket. "Want me to read these to you, so's you can add what you like?" I waved the letters.

Miss Rosie put her hand over mine, then shook her head. "You'll do right by me and my boys, Miss Stella. I knows that."

She had me smiling down to my toes. "Thank you, Miss Rosie. I'll get these off today."

I made to run for the main road as Miss Rosie called after me, "You see my Caleb, send him home direct."

"Yes, ma'am."

Wasn't much for town, so I favored the idea they put the bureau in a shack on the old ginning road. But folks said it just showed the whites didn't put no store by all the work the bureau had to be doing. They spoke true.

That place looked twenty years past ready to fall down, with its leaned-over porch, sagging roof, and broken-out windows, but that didn't stop the folks from coming in, asking for letters to be written. Wanting a way to marry. Looking for food. Asking after work if they be new to the area. Needing help to fight them contracts planters like Hendersen had their children bound up in. Place looked busier than a train station on a holiday.

I posted a notice about Miss Rosie and her boys on the finding board, then I waited in line till it got dark enough for me to wish I'd brung a lantern. Most folks in these parts knew me by sight, so I figured the stares I kept getting came from the folks who'd walked their way to Helensburg from their home place. And who wouldn't stare at a white girl waiting in line at a Freedmen's Bureau?

As I came to the head of the line, the white fella at the table winced. "How can you call yourself a lady walking around like some field hand?"

Seeing's how I spent my day in the field, my appearance seemed right proper, so I just put my letters on the table all folded up and addressed. "You send these?"

He held one up, then looked at another. "Mighty fine penmanship. Who wrote these?"

What on God's green earth did penmanship have to do with the price of cotton in Memphis?

I said, "I want them sent."

Looking bothered, he swiped them into a bag hanging off the edge of the table, saying, "I'll send them." I didn't like the lazy way he said that.

Stopping his hand, I said, "They going to be sent?"

He yanked his hand back, yelling, "They'll go out with all the others!"

I nodded.

"I got me a notice for the newspaper. How I find the right place to send it?"

"Let me see it." He held his hand out all *why-you-got-to-bother-me*, but I gave him the advertisement.

Could feel the folks leaning in to have a look at what I might be about. Filled me with that same fence-sitting feeling that'd been dogging me of late. Felt stuck on that fence like nobody'd let me down on either side. White folks didn't want me stepping foot on their side 'cause I saw black folks as equals and didn't follow all their sissified rules about being a lady. And black folks weren't too keen on me being on their side 'cause of the color of my skin and the sins of my race that had me twenty pounds heavier with the guilt of it all. Hated being on that fence, with folks staring at me from both sides. Wished I could just tear that darn thing down and be done with it.

"Need it to go to the *Christian Recorder*?"

"Yes, sir."

"I'll send it along."

"Thank you, sir."

"You can thank me by keeping to your own kind."

In the end, he'd probably be more thankful if I could blind his mind's eye so he didn't see so crooked, but I just turned and walked off, listening to him mumble on about a white girl gone bad. He should be worrying after his own soul in my way of thinking.

Seeing such a surly white fella working in the bureau seemed a sign of just how hard colored folks had to work to be treated regular in these parts what with the government giving such men bureau jobs and all. What did I have to be whining about in my life when there wasn't a thing that the colored folks did that white folks didn't try to tear down or bury.

Condemning abandoned buildings folks used to start up schools, saying they are unfit for habitation. Then a week later, there's somebody living in the old place like the colored folks had never been studying there—children by day and adults by night for a chance at learning to read and write.

But when one school got shut down, they just opened another. Maggie done taught school in the meeting house on Oak Grove. Over at the Hendersens, Miss Dory helping folks read and write in the tack room. But I've heard tell of schools in barns, storerooms, and cabins from here to the one in Potter's Creek. Weren't no colored folks in these parts going to let no white men have the last say in where they could learn. Time for that sort of nonsense had passed.

And if they'd allowed more of them schools to open, more colored folks would be ready to work in them bureaus, helping other folks track down family, write letters, read forms, know the laws. Now wouldn't that be the right way of things? Of course, that means it wouldn't be happening any too soon.

And just the same, I figured my letters had small chance of reaching their marks, so I went straight back to Daddy's desk and got to writing. Thought I should send the same said letters through the post, along with another advertisement to try to reach that paper direct. That might just about double my chances of finding Miss Rosie's babies. If one of the bureau letters didn't get put up or passed around, the folks at the post office might do it. And when I wasn't writing, I pitched in to do my share of the weeding. Wrote me letters every day. Worked the fields and did my logs. Didn't bother with the meetings on account of knowing the folks wouldn't be putting out no welcome mat for the likes of me.

All that hoeing and writing and writing and hoeing had me so dog tired my body could've slept till Christmas, but come bedtime, I set to praying for my letters to reach Miss Rosie's boys.

Wanted them to find those letters in a post office or a bureau or maybe even hear tell of them among the folks camped along the road as they all headed north. Prayed so hard my own thoughts even went thin and my prayer turned to a chant—*Isaac, Jacob, Abraham*, just started repeating their names like I might be calling them home. *Isaac, Jacob, Abraham.*

Till I could see a man walking a dusty road, shoulders as stooped as the hat sliding low over his eyes. Heard the Lord say, *"The road is long, but he's walking to find his mama, Rosie."*

Sat up so straight and fast, near about lost my breath.

Had I really done it? Had one of my letters actually reached one of Miss Rosie's boys? The idea of it had my heart flip-flopping like a bird on a string. Felt like running to Hattie to tell her what I'd heard, but seeing the blanket twisted around my legs, feeling the sweat on my skin, I knew I'd been dreaming. One of them letters couldn't have reached that far south even if it'd been carried by a real bird, but darn if that wasn't a right good dream.

Good Lord, I prayed it'd come true, but my mind started hearing Richardson crowing, felt sure I'd wake up to his lousy singing, "Five more days to glory, hal-a-loo, hal-a-loo."

Screams beat him to it.

Fire in the Soul

Screams of fear yanked me clean out of bed. Had me in a fright so bad, I near about went through the window, but I ran for the door. Place had the mayhem on it as I came out. Everyone running this way and that, buckets to hand, trying to put out the fire around the house.

Took my mind a bit to take it all in. See them flames. Find my legs to run for a bucket of my own. About then, I saw them. Those men looking like they'd put on the sheets from their beds and cut holes for their eyes. Had crosses in red slashed across their chests and torches in their hands, yelling and setting fire to the grass to complete the ring around the house. I'd heard tell of the Ku Klux Klan burning colored folks off their land, but never did hear tell of them burning out a plantation.

But that ring of fire closing in around the folks trying to put it out, told me I had no time to be thinking. Knew just what to do. All my years of roof-sitting put me in the right mind for this very moment. I went for the back door, ran them steps three at a time. Skidded around the corner as I charged down the hall for Granddaddy's room. Pulled that shotgun off the mantel, grabbed the ammo bag off the door, then went for the stairs to the attic. *Clang* went the door, *pop* went the window on the far end.

Scraped half the skin off my knee crawling out that little window, but I had myself up on that roof in no time. Scanned those men, looking for the fella pointing and shouting orders from his horse. Got me a good aim and *ka-boom!* I split the branch over that low-down dog's head. Sent his horse a-running.

Them men started twisting and turning like ghosts trapped in a graveyard. *Boom!* I shot into the mound holding up the hitching post, sending bits of wood and dirt every which way, making those men do just about the same. When they started running, I reloaded. Shot into the ground behind them, sending up twigs and such when they hit the woods. Reload. Fire. Until every darn one them had run off.

Clean of the Klan, we had a fire to fight.

I ran for the kitchen yard, grabbing a wet blanket from the pile Maggie had started. Set to fighting them flames by slapping them down. Fire snapped and sizzled, but kept coming at me. Got my arms to fanning faster till I thought they'd come clean off. Soon as I put out a flame, had to move after another. And another. Praying all the while, "Lord, don't let this fire burn nobody. Don't let it burn nobody."

"The roof's on fire!" somebody shouted. I turned to see the flames had gone after the west porch.

Didn't give a darn about no roof. Let it burn. Just fight that fire before it gets to burning something that matters.

Seen folks running out of the woods, but this time it was folks from the Hendersen place. Mr. Caleb, Hattie, and Miss Rosie ran right up front, hauling blankets and heading for the well house.

Felt a splash of good cheer to see Mr. Caleb. But there was no time for that.

Could see Mr. Quincy and Mr. Yates hacking at the posts of the porch with axes. Seeing one post standing bare, I grabbed Daddy's ax and set to, but it didn't take no time to see I couldn't keep up to those men. Even Hattie's daddy, Mr. Caleb, seen it. He had that ax out of my hand and himself caught up before Mr. Yates cut through. When Quincy's gave, the flaming roof lurched toward the front lawn.

"It's coming down!" someone shouted.

Good Lord, get clear, Mr. Caleb!

He sidestepped, then tripped as the roof came down.

Dear Lord, no!

Mr. Quincy came running, his hat flying off when he pulled Mr. Caleb clear as that roof hit the ground in a sparking explosion of flame and wood. Both men came away on fire.

I threw that wet blanket on them as fast as I could. Hattie screamed, but set to patting her daddy down to put that fire out. Mr. Quincy and Mr. Caleb rolled and twisted under us.

Miss Rosie came to tend to Mr. Caleb, but he shooed her back to fighting the fire, then followed Mr. Quincy to the well house. Miss Rosie and Hattie set to bucket filling as I went for a fresh blanket. We had more flames to put out.

When the body goes tired before the work be done, the only thing that keeps you going is the soul. You know you got to go on, but your body says it don't have a thing left, so you just pray you a prayer and you push on, the Holy Spirit lighting a fire in your soul to keep you going. And by that light I fought that fire side by side

74

with the folks who prayed right along with me that we could keep it from the cotton.

Come dawn, we had folks dragging themselves off for a few hours' sleep before we went into the fields. The ground around the house looked as black as Mr. Beeman's fire pit. West porch nothing but rubble. The veranda scorched from the pillars to the windows. Saplings out front had been burnt into charred sticks. But the house stood sound.

Standing there staring at that stubborn old place that'd been built when they called Washington "General," I realized it had seen two wars already. Now it faced a third—the fight for Oak Grove itself. And I planned on winning this one.

Coming Clean

Seeing Mrs. Wynston salving up Mr. Quincy's shoulder as he spun his hat in his hand, I felt the pain of it in my own body. Put my mind on Mr. Caleb, so I set out to find Hattie. Poor man came home to save his daughter and ended up nearly losing his life trying to save a house nobody been living in. Of course, if we didn't stop the fire at the house, all the cotton would've gone up like so much chaff in the wind.

Found Hattie helping folks clean up, raking and hauling. Miss Rosie seen me and said, "You girls go on down to the creek and wash up."

As we headed for the creek, I asked, "How's your daddy?"

"Burned more clothes than skin," Hattie said, but she didn't look like she believed it. "That's what he say. But he worked on a broke ankle for days claiming it weren't nothing but a twist."

We had us a dunk in the creek to clean us up, cough out that smoke. "Who you think it was under them sheets?" Hattie asked, rubbing her clothes with a bar a' soap.

I stood beside her, knowing she'd have better luck trying to think of a planter who *didn't* have a dying wish for the folks of Oak Grove.

Any number of the planters in these parts hated Daddy enough to burn his home. Fact that they burned the house and not the quarters or the fields put Richardson top on my list. He didn't want to scare off the folks or ruin a crop he figured to be his in a week. No, he planned on burning me out, so's I'd have nowhere to stay. He didn't need the house, what with his plantation only a mile or so down the road.

I'd heard tell of them burning places down on the river where the fever spread like fire itself. And it just burned me in the gut to think on how that Richardson might've just done it to prevent the fever from spreading. Place ain't got no more fever in it than I do. Or was he so low-down that he burned it so's he could pay less for the place—after all, the house could sell for near to ten thousand its ownself.

"You thinking on Richardson and his men?" All those years standing side by side gave Hattie lots of practice at seeing my thoughts.

I nodded.

Hattie sat right down in the water, her head going under, so she could wash out her hair a little. She came up shaking those braids of hers, then said, "Wasn't it Richardson himself who said, highest compliment you can pay a man is to fear him?"

I rolled my eyes. Sounded like something just foolish enough to be one of the poor excuses for an idea he had rattling around in that dried-up old brain of his.

"Now follow that idea and tell me, what's it mean if a man's afraid of a little ole girl?" She bumped me. We laughed. "Why else would that man be coming through here, singing like he does? That didn't work, so now he's trying to burn you out. He's afraid of what you going to do next."

When I said nothing, her wet hands went to her soapy hips and she asked, "And just what are you going to do?"

I gave her the *wait-and-see* look.

She huffed and set back to scrubbing. "Well, I'm plumb tired of those white people making my parents wait. Papa went down to the bureau so's they can declare that contract Hendersen have on me illegal. Why, they told Papa they'd have to write to some fella upstate to get a ruling. Meantime, they want Papa to find his marriage license 'cause that goes to show he's my papa. Why we got to prove anything when Hendersen be the one writing up papers and lying?"

Weren't no reason to it.

"It's just white people protecting white people. That's what it is."

Hattie weren't wrong. But her words had me wondering just what she saw when she looked at me.

"Am I white?"

"You are now you got all the soot off you," Hattie said, rubbing a bit off my face.

"Am I white like them white people protecting white people?"

Hattie backed up. "What you asking me, Stella?"

I hated to see that look in Hattie's eye. That spark of mistrust with a hint of fear and a lot of anger. I've seen it time and time again when a colored person is testing the waters, waiting to see what a white person's going to do. That answered me right quick.

I turned to walk out of the water, my heart just a drowning in the idea that that fence I'd been sitting on cut right through the friendship between me and Hattie. Built up by the world around us, weren't much I could do to take it down.

Hattie sloshed out of that water and spun me around. "I said, what you asking me, Stella?"

That spin had my head kind of light. "I look at you, I see Hattie. What you see in me?"

"A crazy girl named Stella, that's what." Hattie gave me a push. "You got any idea how I defend you? Folks saying I shouldn't be spending my time with no white girl."

Hattie had me by the heart and she was twisting.

"People saying you ain't right in the head." She put her hand to her chest. "I defend you, Stella Reid, sunrise to moonrise, so don't go doubting me now."

She gave me another push. "You hear me, Stella?"

I nodded, feeling kind of swimmy. Didn't seem to have enough air to take in what Hattie had said. When I tripped on the way back, Hattie asked me, "You all right, Stella?"

My swooning must've answered her, 'cause she grabbed my arm and pulled me over to a bench, saying, "Girl, you done run yourself down. We got to get you to bed." She shouted, "Mrs. Wynston, help me with Miss Stella!"

"That girl finally admitting she's human?" Mrs. Wynston crossed the kitchen yard. Taking my left arm, Mrs. Wynston waited for Hattie to take the right, then led the way to Daddy's office, saying, "Jumping on that roof and taking shots at those fools like they rabbits. Whacking that fire back like it weren't nothing more than a possum. Taking an ax to the house like some lumberjack." She laughed, opening the office door. "Miss Stella, you is as wild with your ways as your daddy." She eased me onto the bed and pulled a quilt up over me. "May the Lord keep you from his end."

With a kiss to my forehead, Mrs. Wynston shooed Hattie out the door, Hattie saying, "You going to let her sleep in them wet clothes?"

"Hush" is all I heard before sleep carried me off.

Setting Things Right

I dreamt of flames and a rooster with Richardson's head until Mr. Beeman's voice pulled me to his shop as he called for me. "Stella, Stella! Help me. I cain't find it. Cain't find it."

In my dream, I saw him on the floor of his shop sifting through the dirt with his hands. I stood over him, waiting for him to tell me what he was looking for. He stared up at me, his face heavy with panic. "I cain't find my money. You seen my money?"

Sat up in bed, knowing that money waited right under me, looking as blood red as if he'd bled on it himself.

I got right up and took it out. Marched down to Mr. Garrett's cabin, that money feeling as light as grass in my hand.

Young Hugh opened the door. "Daddy, it's Miss Stella."

Mr. Garrett came round his son to have a look. "Morning, Miss Stella. You be needing something."

I held out the money.

"This for us?" He took that money like I offered him a brand-new baby.

"From your daddy."

Mr. Garrett dropped into the chair, his arms limp as the

money that sat in his lap. He'd probably never seen that kind of money, let alone owned it. "How?"

"Raised it. Buy him a shop."

Henry got off the bed to come stand behind his father.

"Can we use it to buy land, Daddy?" Hugh asked, putting his hand out, but too timid to touch the money.

Mr. Garrett closed his eyes and shook his head, whispering, "Daddy."

And the ache that echoed in my heart told me I knew just how he felt. I backed out of there to leave those folks with the only gift Mr. Beeman could give them now.

Even with the sun climbing in the sky, not too many folks moved about, the air hung thick with the smell of soot. Wasn't a soul on the place that didn't need their rest.

Walking by their doors, seeing their windows dark, I felt soul-thin to realize they might be losing their very beds come auction time. Richardson wouldn't make nothing easy for the folks who'd worked for my daddy. Wouldn't put it past Richardson to not even allow folks to take things out of their cabins, claiming they's his. And Mr. Quincy'd lose the place he'd built for his family.

Felt ready to bury myself under quilts and wait for the mighty Rooster Richardson to crow his way by, but I walked by the safe and had to have another crack at it. This time I chose the day Daddy'd finished the meeting house and held the first meeting inside. He even took the time to carve the date over the door. Felt sure I had it this time.

Left to 1, right past 4, then back. Did I hear a click? Please, Lord. On to 54. Pull.

Nothing.

A knock at the door startled the disappointment right out of me. Found Mr. Beeman's Garrett on my stoop.

"I been musing, Miss Stella." He turned the knob on the door as he held it. Had me thinking his mind must be twisting and turning just like that creaky old knob. "As I figure it, my daddy started raising this money a long time ago. So he must've been saving it up to buy me and my boys free." He smiled over the idea.

Didn't see no need for him to be telling me this truth, so I just waited.

"Right?" He looked at me, the guilt and worry pulling at his eyes until they teared up.

I nodded.

His shoulders lifted like he felt lighter. "Then they's no need for other folks to know we got this here money, right?"

I agreed.

"Good." He sighed. Then he kicked the stoop, asking, "You think there'd be any chance they'd be selling off the shops? You know, Harris's woodworking. Daddy's smithy."

"Separatelike?"

He nodded.

"Near as I figure, they don't plan on breaking off anything but the fallow land. 'Less of course they don't get no bidders on the plantation proper. But Richardson'll see that don't happen."

"But he have him a smithy down the road at his place. What he be wanting my daddy's for?"

"You thinking of smithing?"

He held his hands out. "Daddy always said God done give me metal-working hands."

"Weren't a better teacher than your daddy." I could see the two of them standing over the fire, Mr. Beeman guiding his son's hands, talking slow and even, like they weren't doing nothing more dangerous than shoeing a horse.

"There's a true tell." He smiled. Looking over his shoulder toward his daddy's shop, he said, "Sure would like to see that shop stay in the family. Ain't a thing in it my daddy didn't put his mark on."

Idea had my heart closing up. Knew just what he meant. Why, Oak Grove had the same kind of meaning for me—a straight line between the here and the now and my daddy. My mama too. If I had my way, that shop would stay in Beeman hands as long as they cared to own it, but I'd given my word to Mr. Vinson. Couldn't make no promises, so I turned Mr. Garrett to a good promise-keeper.

"You should pray on it." God would tell him what to do.

He smiled. "Now that be a fine idea, Miss Stella. I sure enough been doing a lot that lately." He laughed, then walked off. From a ways away, he yelled back, "Besides, they got them plenty of smithies up north, now, don't they."

That money could've bought a hundred and twenty more acres, but giving his kin a chance at the future Mr. Beeman wanted them to have seemed worth more right about then. Felt good to be a small part of a father passing something on to his son and grandsons.

Made me remember I had my daddy's promise to try and keep. And Mr. Garrett's worry over secrets made me realize I had no reason to keep any from Mr. Vinson, so I went to tell him what I had in mind.

He had himself an office behind his house. He left the door open to give folks the sign they could come in. I knocked on the jamb.

"Miss Stella." He didn't look up, just kept figuring. Daddy taught him reading, writing, and figuring when Mr. Vinson first come to Oak Grove. Now he probably did it better than Daddy ever could. I tried to do the same with Daddy's log book.

"Been thinking on giving a Yankee money to outbid Richardson."

Mr. Vinson dropped his pencil and stood up, staring at me like I said I planned to try my hand at flying. "Come again, Miss Stella?"

"You buy the fallow land. Richardson'll buy Oak Grove. You don't want him close."

"So you're giving your daddy's money to some stranger?" He shook his head. "Miss Stella, you best be keeping that money. It'll do you fine to buy land of your own. Attract you a good husband."

I didn't want no stupid husband. I wanted Oak Grove.

"He can't have it."

Mr. Vinson sighed and rubbed his neck. "Miss Stella, I can't be telling you what to do, I ain't your kin, but I got to tell you, this sounds like a fool's plan to me. You don't know this Yankee you'll be trusting."

I felt the flood of foolishness wash over me. What had I been thinking? Why would I trust some stranger to bid on Oak Grove and not just take my money and push me out into the road?

Only a fool mistakes her own idea for one sent from the Lord. I prayed God would forgive me, but He said, *"Put your trust in me."*

Now that'd be about right. If I trusted the Lord to lead me to just the right Yankee, I might could pull this off.

Mr. Vinson had gone back to his desk. Right about then, I realized he'd been counting. Counting up the money he'd been collecting from folks for the auction.

I stood next to his desk. "You can leave this fool to her ideas, but it looks like you all have a good stake."

He laughed and shook his head. "Well, we still got a week now. But we ain't got more than twelve hundred so far."

He sounded as uncertain as I felt. That called for prayer because they needed their money as much as I needed mine. In fact, I could use a good bit more, so I nodded him good night, then headed back to the office for a think.

Seeing that safe again, I wished it was filled with money and I could think up that combination, then the folks of Oak Grove could get their land and I could find me a Yankee to buy the rest of the place and we'd be free and clear.

What a dream. Felt like blowing that darn safe up. But Daddy had ordered it special to have the strongest kind they built. Seller said the last fellas who tried to blow up one of them safes had to use so much dynamite, they blew up the safe *and* the money inside.

Couldn't think of another important date, so I tried something silly, birthday of daddy's horse, Old Valiant, 3-8-56. Nothing. Why did I even bother?

Wrote the log, then set to wandering, to wait on a sign from the Good Lord that I was headed in the right direction. Just prayed and thought and prayed until I found myself in Mama's garden, sitting on her thinking rock.

Remembered what Mr. Vinson said about finding myself a husband. Made me think on how Mama worried after the very same affair. But I never thought much on me being a wife or a mama in my own right. Wouldn't be good at it. More likely to turn the poor child as fool crazy as me. Mama tried to school me up right on music lessons, reading, table manners, all that, but I favored tree climbing, weed pulling, and britches.

Heard her more than once, whispering to herself, "Give her time to grow," like I was one of her little flowers, and if she gave me time enough, I'd grow into a lady like her—but weren't no one like Mama.

Mama tended me like one of her flowers in many ways. Not just in the day-to-day loving of her life, but she had what she called a trousseau, a trunk she did up for when I got married, sewed her a quilt for my wedding bed, put in a sliver platter for my table, thing looked more like a mirror to me and I'd never been one to bother with them things. Now wait, a memory had me on my feet.

Come the talk of war, Mama done had Daddy put a false bottom in that trunk. And she put a few things inside there. What if she tucked away something I could sell? I ran for that house fast as a rabbit. My usual route had come down in the fight to stop the fire, so I went for the trellis on the far side and come up onto the veranda by my parents' room.

Stood over that table I used to hide under, feeling all funny. Thing looked too small. Couldn't hardly hide my legs under there now. And staring in that room all dark and dusty, felt like I looked into a hollow of the past, carved out of all the life it used to hold.

Couldn't bring myself to go in through there, so I went to the doors that opened into the hallway, then up the stairs to the attic. Found my trunk all buried under old rugs and blankets and such—Mama hiding it from Yankee eyes, no doubt.

The lid near about opened with a pop, letting out a cloud of cedar and talc, the elder flower talc Mama used. Making me close my eyes against a wave that passed through me, all thoughts on Mama and loneliness. Sat there rubbing her quilt, seeing her hands working in and out, wanting to touch them, feeling her fingers tracing mine as she told me a bedtime story, seeing that rise in the cheek smile of hers.

Put that quilt over my shoulders to feel her close and set to digging for that false bottom. Found it too. Darn, how I wished it were just as easy to get into Daddy's safe. Idea had me eager, wishing, praying Daddy might've thought to hide them papers in that trunk. He'd probably figure we'd look there. I ran my hand through that bottom so fast and hard I scraped my knuckles, finding a box and paper. I found paper.

I yanked it out and started reading like my next breath depended on it. But it was just one of them darn blame letters of introduction saying Mama wanted some fancified lady in Natchez to host my coming-out cotillion and could she sell some silly old necklace to pay for the affair.

Made me feel a bit like Mama done tried to reach into the future to see me safe in a time she'd never see. Said my thanks to her, then had a look in the box at the very necklace her letter talked on—an ugly old thing with a string of fancy gems look like a bunch of stars stolen from the sky and crushed down. Never did like jewelry. Always made me think of stars trapped around somebody's neck, just wanted to rip them off and set them free.

But that there necklace might just buy me a little piece of Oak Grove. Box in hand, I headed back to the office, praying the Lord would show me just what I should do next. And if He had any ideas on dates I could try with that safe, I sure would appreciate it. I thought I heard a laugh. Did God laugh? If he did, he probably thought it was really funny how a foolish little girl such as myself thought I could hold on to a plantation like Oak Grove. Now that's a right funny idea.

Time Do Tell

"Four more days to glory, hal-a-loo, hal-a-loo. Four more days to glory, hal-a-loo." Richardson didn't start singing until he got well past our place that morning. Probably figured I might be ready with my shotgun again. Each day, he rode up, crowed his crow, then rode off fast and hard. Set to wishing I had Old Valiant under me, he'd a' run that lame old horse down and show it a thing or two, but I couldn't do nothing but outrun that Richardson.

Had myself lost in them kind of thoughts when Mrs. Wynston called to me from the edge of the field, "Miss Stella, you got you a visitor at the house."

I stared at her like she'd said the governor'd come calling. I didn't never have no visitors.

"It's Miss Katherine Shaw."

Cousin Mertle's nurse. *What did she want?* Richardson probably sent her out to nudge me into moving townward. Leaving my hoe against the office, I headed on into the house. Didn't like the staleness of it. Smelled like old wax and dusty fabric. Found Miss Shaw in the sitting room all hands in her lap at the tea table.

She stood and did a little bow like she'd come for a party or something. "Miss Stella."

Didn't feel like talking to nobody, especially not the likes of her. Never did feel right about a body who spent her life taking care of a woman she didn't share a drop a blood or an ounce of love with. Seemed like a kind of a gold-digging a body did without a pick. Other folks called it Christian charity, but I seen she wasn't in it for kindness' sake.

"I come to talk with you about Miss Mertle."

Well, I didn't figure she came to talk cotton prices.

She forced a smile, the kind folks used to hide clenched teeth. "Mr. Richardson tells me they'll be selling Oak Grove. He said you should be moving into town with your cousin. Well, I would never dream of turning away an orphan such as yourself. But as you know, Miss Mertle is getting on in years."

"Getting on"? Daddy says she was old when he came into this here world. She had to be as old as a rock by now.

"And she can't do for herself like she used to."

Folks said she tended to nap during meals and needed to be roused to finish.

"Now, I wouldn't feel the least bit put out to look after you." The smile she put on looked like it hurt.

I didn't need no looking after. Who did she think been seeing after me since Mama took sick? The dogs?

"But I just wanted things to be clear before you come on. You are Miss Mertle's only living relative that's for certain, but I need to clarify that I've been nursing her since I was but your age. Now that my marrying years are behind me, I have to expect to be taken care of by your family in payment for all my years of service."

Like I said, gold-digging without a pick.

Told her, "Shouldn't have to live without love."

She bowed her head, saying, "I have made some sacrifices."

"I meant Miss Mertle." After all, she'd married herself a husband and they'd had themselves three children. They all died in the yellow fever of '14, leaving her alone and loveless.

"I never." Miss Katherine stood up all stifflike. "Are you trying to say I haven't done right by your cousin? Why, I've cleaned up after that old woman for more years than you've been alive. I just want what I'm owed."

What she's owed was a good long lesson on love. Folks who do such a thing for money must have souls thin enough to blow away in the wind. Maybe that's why they're after gold—figure it'll weigh them down.

"I'm talking to you, Miss Stella Reid. Do you hear me?"

Oh, no, she'd gone to shouting, making my ears hurt, so I had to give them a rub.

She stomped her foot, huffed, and snapped her head to the side like a filly that'd been saddled wrong. "You are the most disagreeable young lady I have ever laid eyes on." Stepping toward the door, she said, "And if folks would listen to me, they'd send you away like they should've done long ago."

She meant one of them hospital sort of places where they locked folks away for not having what they called a "right" mind. What I wanted to know is why they didn't have places for folks who weren't right in the heart.

"Can't all have what we want," I said, opening the door.

She stormed out of there like I'd set fire to her skirt, saying, "Well, you can just find yourself another place to stay for all I care."

I had me a place to stay. And though it made her mad enough to take the clippers to that oaf Hendersen's prized yellow rose bush, so did Hattie.

"Papa spent near about every waking night tracking down that lieutenant what married them to get a copy of that certificate they stole, only to wait in line all day at the bureau today again," she said, lopping off roses in full bloom. "All day. Then he had to work till dawn to fill all the orders Hendersen had waiting on him." *Snip. Snip.* She'd gone to cutting branches.

I thought of telling her about my dream on her brother walking to find his mama, but it didn't seem like the right time with the way she working them shears, all anger and snapping like a bear trap.

Pointing the shears at me, she said, "Hendersen done talked to those bureau folks, I just know it. Now they saying Papa need him a letter of employment."

Chop. Chop. Wasn't much left of that bush by now. "Hendersen say he won't write one. Well, Papa's had him enough. Come sundown on Friday, Mama and Papa going up to the Adams County Courthouse to have a talk with some uppity-up at the bureau. But it'll take them half the night to get there. Don't know what I'll do if they come home without no good news." Shaking her head, she gave that bush one more good *chop*. "I just don't know, Stella. Don't know atall. I'm going to be cutting this here rose bush until I'm too old to see."

Not if there's nothing left of it.

"Girl!" Mrs. Hendersen shouted from a window above. Had Hattie jumping like she'd seen a snake. "What have you done to my husband's rosebush?"

93

"There's a nasty bug, eating all the leaves. Had to cut it back to save it, ma'am."

"I see." She tried to look closer to test Hattie's lie. When she couldn't see enough to tell, she said, "Well, why don't you pick some white ones for his room. He still isn't feeling well today."

"Yes, ma'am."

Mrs. Hendersen went inside and Hattie hauled me around the corner of the house, so she could laugh free and clear of Mrs. Hendersen's sensitive ears. Catching her breath after a good belly laugh, Hattie said, "That root sure is doing its job." She smiled. "Best get to those flowers, but I think I might go pick from those nice rosebushes down by your mama's hives. You think I might find me one with a pretty old bee in it?"

That Hattie had herself a copperhead streak. She struck so fast and quick you didn't see it coming. But I did hope Miss Rosie and Mr. Caleb got that bureau fellow to declare that contract illegal like he should.

Funny how Hattie couldn't wait for Saturday to come to see if her parents could get her free of Hendersen, and I dreaded it, what with old Richardson and his song drumming in my head, "A few more days to glory." Boo-hoo in my way of thinking. But the days just kept a-coming. So I had to do something and I figured a trip to good old Cousin Mertle seemed in order.

A Hint of Hope

Miss Mertle had herself one a' them fine houses in town with the colored glass windows and the half circle balcony over the door held up by columns, looking like a big ole fancy wedding cake.

Standing on the stoop, I pulled at the dress it took me near to an hour to find in Mama's wardrobe. Never did figure out them darn hoops, so I used a riding dress, but I only had my own boots to wear. My big draft-horse feet didn't even fit into Mama's slippers, let alone her shoes. But I looked a might better than a field hand when I knocked with the old ring hanging out of the mouth of the lion old Cousin Mertle had stuck to her door.

That prickly Katherine Shaw answered the door, saying, "And just what would you be wanting, Miss Reid?"

"Who's there?" Miss Mertle called from inside, sounding startled.

Well, I sure didn't come to discuss the weather, but I figured I'd better play nice or that woman wouldn't let me in the house.

Holding up the box I brought, I said, "Found something Miss Mertle might like to have a look at."

"What is it?" Miss Shaw said, her voice going high and light, her eyes all *what-you-got-there*.

"I *said*, who is there?" Now Miss Mertle sounded downright mad.

"It's Stella Reid, Miss Mertle."

"Why, child, get yourself inside. It's a frightful heat out there."

In Miss Mertle's mind women shouldn't be exposed to heat. They're too delicate. *Phew.* By that rule, I'd never go outside. I grabbed my hankie to give myself a wipe down so she couldn't see my sweat, then stepped around Miss Shaw—who went all shuffling feet to get to the parlor before me and announce, "Miss Stella Reid," like I done stopped for a visit to the queen or something.

Miss Mertle sat in a chair, all full dress with a collar up to her chin, a fancy cloth over her bunned-up hair, lacy little gloves, and all. No wonder she worried after the heat. Why, a cold-blooded snake'd be downright hot in that getup. She looked like a doll to me, except for the wrinkles. Made me wonder why they never did make any dolls that look like old folks. After all, they needed just as much looking after as any baby.

"And what brings you into town, Miss Stella? Here to talk about your schooling?"

Miss Mertle done told Mama I should be sent to one of them finishing schools, but I wanted to know just what they thought they could finish on what God started. I figure He made me the way I'm meant to be and that's that.

"No, ma'am. Came to show this." I handed her the box, open on account of her hands aren't so capable anymore.

"My," she said, putting her hand to her chest. "I do remember this." She stroked it like it might be one of them little, yippy lapdogs she's so fond of. "Your mother wore it the night of her cotillion. She looked to be a vision in it." She sat up straight and smiled real big with the memory of it. "Your father near about melted, waiting on her hand to foot, hoping she'd take a liking to him."

Wished I'd a been there to see them courting. But only for the chance to see them. I'm not one for courting. Folks are all flutter this and flutter that, never really saying anything straight or true, talking all honey and wine. Makes my stomach sour just thinking on it. So maybe I'm just as lucky that I never did have to see all that between Mama and Daddy.

"And why have you brought it to me, Stella?"

The way she pet that thing made me worry that maybe she'd been the one to give it to Mama. If that'd been the case, I'd be asking her to buy it twice if I tried to sell it to her like I planned on doing. "You give that to my mama?"

"Heavens, no." She laughed. "My cousin Henrietta, your grandmother, married into the Carter family. This belonged to her husband's mother, I believe. It's quite old." She winked at me. "Even older than me."

I held my breath to hold back a laugh, then I said, "But you like it?"

"Like it?" She turned her head and squinted her eyes, trying to decide just what I might be about. "Are you looking to sell this, Stella?"

I nodded.

She snapped that box shut so fast I thought it'd break. "This is not an item to be sold, Miss Reid. It's an heirloom. Do you know what that means?"

Not for certain, but she was fixing to tell me.

"It's a piece of your family history and you can't be selling it like some heifer you have no need for."

"Oak Grove is my family history."

She sighed, her hands closed over the box. "So, that's what this is about. You want to try to keep that land in your family."

"Near as I can."

She pulled her eyelids back in shock. "But you're just a young woman. What can a lady as young as yourself do with a plantation?"

Miss Shaw, who'd been waiting at the door like a maid, stepped in, saying, "Miss Reid, you are upsetting your cousin. Perhaps you should leave."

"Wait." Cousin Mertle put a hand to stop Miss Shaw from coming to collect me. "Just what do you have in mind, Stella?"

I closed my eyes, knowing Cousin Mertle hated Yankees about as much as she hated colored folks. She wouldn't understand what I had in mind. She'd hate it, really, so I had to put things in such a way that she'd be for the idea. And I decided to go for her third biggest hate, Daniel Richardson, the man who tried to buy her house out from under her when she took sick a year or so back.

"Plan on making sure a bidder goes higher than Richardson to buy me a stake in the place."

That a lit a spark in her eye. "Clever, girl. You plan to keep the place out of that greedy man's hands and make a place for yourself in the bargain."

"Yes, ma'am."

"And just how much would you be needing to do this?" She sat up straight, looking all *see-here*.

That question had Miss Shaw stepping forward all nervouslike and unsure of what to do. Her little rabbit dance didn't get past Miss Mertle, who narrowed her eyes and said, "Katherine, bring me my sewing."

Sewing? What did she need to sew right now?

"Yes, ma'am," said Katherine, looking like she'd just lost her own dog. She left the room.

"Miss Stella?"

"I got me a thousand. Not sure how much more I'll be needing, but the place may go for—"

"Miss Stella!" She spoke so sharp and quick, she made me jump. "Your grammar is worse than that of a colored girl. And a woman never discusses money in such a way. She merely hints."

How's a girl get what she wants if she just hints?

I put on my best book language and said, "Well, ma'am. I will take what you are willing to offer me."

"That's better." Miss Mertle took the sewing basket Miss Shaw brought. My cousin had her eyes on me, so she didn't see that *I-hope-you-die* look that Miss Shaw gave me. "Now, I will give you a package. And you won't open it or count it until you get home, like a proper young lady. And you'll send whoever purchases the place to me. I'll make very clear that I've invested in the place to ensure you're properly cared for and well-schooled." She reached inside, keeping the hinges to me, so I couldn't see a thing, except a stiff little package wrapped in brown paper and tied up in string like one a' them bars of chocolate little Vera loved so much.

She handed it to me, saying, "Do we have an understanding, Stella?"

"Yes, ma'am." I closed my hands over it best I could and did a curtsey like I knowed I should.

"Very good, child." She smiled and snapped that box shut. "And I'll keep this necklace for your cotillion."

"Thank you, ma'am," I said, backing up, knowing from the grasping look on Miss Shaw's face that'd she'd do everything she could to be sure I never saw that necklace again.

Didn't matter none to me. I had me a much better package to take home and I done that at a run, cutting between buildings and heading into the trees soon as I could before Richardson caught sight of me and set to wondering what I had in mind.

Ran straight to Daddy's office and even locked the door before I had a look inside that package. Found me a whole stack of them big stiff bills banks done give out, all fancy and looking like they'd never been touched. Felt funny to count them, like it might be doing something wrong, but I counted and recounted and realized she'd done given me two thousand dollars.

No wonder that Miss Shaw acted like a big old dog guarding a bag a gold. My cousin Mertle done sitting in that old house with a bank in her darn sewing box. *Whoo-hee.* Felt like gold to me.

Even thought on dancing, felt so happy to have that money and a chance to beat old Richardson at his own game. *Well, a cock-a-doodle-dumb-dumb to you, Richardson.*

By Faith

By the time Friday came around, my nerves had wound my muscles up so tight I couldn't sit still, not even after a day of hoeing fast enough to clear me a half a dozen rows by sundown. Carting water to folks, Mr. Jasper said, "We could hitch up to Miss Stella today and travel to the stars."

Folks laughed, but I just kept hoeing.

After supper I paced, trying date after date on that darn blame safe until I felt ready to beat my fists to pulp on that thing. Come nightfall, Mr. Vinson knocked on my door. Looking around, he said, "You opening one of them museums I hear tell of over in Washington City?"

My mind didn't catch on to his meaning before he said, "Place looks like your daddy just left."

"Daddy could never leave here altogether." I sat up.

Rubbing the edge of Daddy's desk, Mr. Vinson said, "True enough." He took up the log book and looked through the pages. I kept it real particular, doing sketches of my maps before I put them in there, making sure my writing looked real nice. But I got all nervous when folks looked at it, afraid they'd see how bad I did.

"A work of art, Miss Stella."

He had my jaw dropping. Art's that fancy kind of stuff they put on walls, not my scratchings.

"This is honest-to-goodness art. Look at them pictures you drew of the leaves that had them weevils, and you make that new well we dug by the garden look mighty fine."

"It ain't nothing."

He set it down and gave it a pat. "Your daddy would think it's right fine."

That put a smile on my face with roots that went to my belly.

"Yes, ma'am." He had another look around, but this time, he eyed the floor more than anywhere else, telling me he'd set to wondering how much of Daddy's stashaway I'd found.

"Nine hundred and fifty seven."

He teased, "You can count that high?"

He only joked when he had a case of nerves, so I waited for them to settle enough for him to say what else he had on his mind.

"Well, I hear you went a-visiting your cousin Mertle. She doing well?" Mr. Vinson did mean well by her, but he also wanted to know more than that, and when I didn't answer, he told me what. "You fixing on moving there?"

"She's helping me stay on here."

"I see." He nodded. "She looking to buy the place?"

I shook my head. "Just give me a bit of help. That's all."

He tried to hide it, but that gave him a bit of a smile. Still feared I might buy that land out from under them. Made me feel small, but I'd have to erase all of the evil the whites in these parts had done to the colored folk to come up even. So I just asked, "And how's your collecting coming?"

"Hmm." He looked behind him. "We got us a fair bit."

"Ain't it peculiar, you got your money, I got mine. Too bad we didn't have enough together to buy this whole place."

"True enough." He sighed, giving the safe a soft kick. "Would you really divide the place up like your daddy planned?"

"Like he planned."

Daddy meant for each family to own their plots, but sell their cotton together, putting in equal to their acreage for seed and gin maintenance and such. Everything divided equal with people paying what the plantation paid, no big markups like the planters do to the sharecroppers. And the profit would be divided by acreage.

Daddy was one to share his food, but not give away his plate, so he planned on keeping about two hundred and forty acres for himself. He wanted to bring on hired hands to work the cotton and turn his attention to raising and training horses like he'd always planned on doing.

Not sure if his take on these things was fair by fair's sake—I never was one to put my mind around big ideas like that—but didn't nobody argue over it when he told folks his plan before he died. Of course, they might have had a thing or two to say in their own homes. But I'd never hear tell of that.

He shook his head. "We was so close." He gripped his hand. "Like I could feel the land in my fist."

"And you're close again."

"We can't buy enough for all the folks here." He scuffed the floor.

Mr. Vinson had that right. There weren't enough acres in that fallow land for more than five or so families. Not to mention it stood fallow because we'd worked the cotton out of it, and the earth needed time to heal up and get good an' healthy again.

"Well, I hope to find me a fellow who'll hire on those who couldn't buy into the land you bidding on."

He raised his eyebrows real slowlike. "Do tell."

"Richardson'd run folks off. But I plan to find me a bidder who will hire on anybody who'd like to stay."

The dullness I seen in his eyes said I spoke true on Richardson, but my plan didn't have enough of the same said truth to give him any hope. "You think you'll find a man who don't have sharecropping in mind?"

"I'm leaving that up to the Good Lord who can find just who we need."

Mr. Vinson smiled at me. "I've prayed all my days for that kind of faith, child."

Had me blushing like I done stepped into a fire. He talked on it like I had some true special gift when I's only talking about all I've known between me and God.

"God said I'd stay to Oak Grove and I aim to see that through."

He laughed. "And I believe you just might."

Crossing the room, he gave the safe another soft kick, saying, "Nothing yet?"

"Stubborn as a mule. Twice as hard to handle." I guess that old saying of Mama's fit for the safe and for me.

"Miss Gayle Anne." He shook his head with a *hmm-hmm* of a good cooking sound. "Boy, could I use some of her okra stew."

Okra tasted like spit in a squeaky green jacket to me, but Mama did know how to cook just about anything. Even got me to eat spinach once. But just once.

He looked out the window into the fading light. "I sure do miss them two."

"Miss Daddy, walk the stalls. Miss Mama, walk the garden."

He smiled down at me. "You may have your mama's wisdom and your daddy's strength, but that mouth of yours is all your own."

The idea of me being a stitched-up quilt of part Mama, part Daddy, and a good chunk of just plain old me, gave me such a heart-happy feeling.

After all, Mama was a fine woman of silks and piled-up hair. Daddy, he stood tall in any saddle he stepped into. Me, I prefer to ride bareback, and silk gives me hives. Thought most of my life that Hattie had been right all along. Mama and Daddy done found me under a bush. But maybe I'd taken in parts of them you never could see.

Mr. Vinson squeezed my shoulder, saying, "They'd be proud, Miss Stella. Real proud."

"And tomorrow?"

"If you pull this plan of yours off, they'd be even prouder then." He smiled so big I could near about see around his teeth. But I didn't feel it none.

I kicked the safe. "You sure you don't know what papers Daddy kept in this thing?"

"Not my business." He just looked out of that window.

I nodded. "Say, what day you come to Oak Grove?"

"You tried that one already. Why's it got to be a date anyhow?"

"Daddy liked his dates." Daddy believed in marking the time something got done. He carved the finishing date in every building he put up—the meeting house, the new gin, the added stalls in the stables. Every one a' them had the date Daddy pounded in the final nail carved over its door.

"Your daddy was a date man." Mr. Vinson smiled. "Even put your walking date in your cradle to mark the last time you slept in it."

Forgot about that there date. Used that cradle for my dolls. But I hadn't touched a doll since I picked up a hoe back when Hattie had to start working. Figured if she had to work, I should too.

But Mr. Vinson had him a good idea. I gave it a try. 8. Nothing. 17. Not a thing. 52. And more of nothing. Obviously, Daddy didn't take no more store in that date than I did. Never did take to celebrating myself in such a way.

Mr. Vinson patted the safe. "Don't mean to be dashing no hopes, but don't you be forgetting your daddy cleaned this here safe for Yankees and militia alike. Why you think he had so much money stashed around?"

I nodded. But Mr. Vinson had it right. Daddy knew any safe'd be a target to looters. Bet he never figured our whole place'd be looted like it would be come auction time. People walking all over it. Looking in this and that, talking on what they saw like they're sizing up a horse, not somebody's home.

"Miss Stella, I know neither of us ain't got much money, but if you have just one thread of faith, you got the world."

I'd heard Mr. Vinson say this before, but I wanted to hear it again.

He obliged. "The Lord Jesus could make himself enough blankets to cover up every chile under the moon with one thread." He tapped my nose. "Don't you go forgetting that."

I nodded.

"'Night now."

Just watched him head on down the path, then I said a prayer in the hopes Jesus might bless our money, theirs and mine, in a fishes-and-loaves kind of way while we slept. That is, if I could sleep.

Put myself into bed, but my mind just kept searching the place, trying to think of some old hidey-hole I hadn't looked in for money, until I sat up and said loud as a bell, "Lord, what you want me to do?"

Lord's not one to go flapping at the mouth. Something I always respected. Seemed to me, people only meant about one out of every ten words that came out of their mouths, so why say them at all? The Good Lord meant every word He uttered, but most folks didn't want to hear them, so He said them where a person shouldn't be able to deny them, straight in the soul. Too bad some folks lived a life that hardened their soul up until they couldn't even hear their own conscience, let alone God.

I set to praying to hear what God had to say on the auction, but all I seen was feet. Worn-out old brown boots a-slapping down their loose soles, just walking down a dirt road. Then I heard a whisper, a cracking voice, saying, "I'm coming, Mama. I'm coming."

Those words chilled my very bones. Had me pulling the quilt around me and fighting back the tears. Good Lord, let that be one of Miss Rosie's boys. Knew by the weight of that wish in my heart that I could never tell Miss Rosie. If I didn't see that tell true, she'd be waiting on a boy that never came. I just couldn't do that to her. Not someone so soul-sweet as Miss Rosie. She deserved to have that boy right there in front of her, hugging her close.

So, I just set right back to praying, thanking the Lord for that sight and asking him to guide my own two feet come the morning. I tried so hard my ears started ringing. Kept thinking I heard, in a feeling kind of way, the same thing over and over, *"Find the man who needs what you have."*

Now, I'm not one to tell God His business, but that didn't make no sense. I didn't have nothing. But when I asked for a little clarifying, God just repeated Himself.

So I stuck that feather in my cap and tried to wear it proud, knowing the Good Lord had a plan, even if I didn't understand it. I'd find myself a Yankee who planned on bidding, then buy me a stake in the place with enough money to let him outbid Richardson.

Must've believed in the message the Good Lord sent me 'cause I actually slept until the sun come up and that rooster of a fool, Richardson, rode by to shout, "Auction's today, Stella Reid! Be gone by selling time!"

I planned on being there come selling time. Right there next to Richardson, watching him lose the bid for Oak Grove. I knew he'd just shrivel up and die if we had even the smallest piece of the place. But first I had to find me a Yankee to bid for us. Seemed right peculiar to be searching up the very men we'd been fearing for so many years.

Yankees Come to Town

During the war, towns like Holly Springs, Mississippi, changed hands more times than a fort has bullets, being captured and recaptured so fast townspeople had trouble knowing whose hands they was in. Became like figuring the weather, with people asking, "Are we under the gray skies again?" And gray skies were a good thing to people in such towns, if you catch my meaning.

Other towns, like Vicksburg, fought to the last man to keep the Yankees out, but still others, like Natchez herself, turned things over like they might be passing the hat for collection come Sunday. Seeing a proud and beautiful city like Vicksburg blown to bits can put the fear of preservation into some folks. And up Natchez way, they sought to save their homes and let the soldiers sort it out on the battlefield elsewhere.

But many a town like our Helensburg fell like a poor animal being tortured by hunters—young boys gone sick in the head with the power of the gun, shooting one leg out from under the animal, then another, not letting it die, but forcing it to feel the pain. That's how Helensburg went down. Yankees came in the spring of 1863, swarming over plantations like hornets, taking cattle, looting smokehouses, ransacking offices for gold, then setting fire to the place for their last sting.

Planters got dragged off to the Vicksburg jail or fined or beaten. Not to mention the awful things that befell their wives. Those Yankees took what they wanted, destroyed what they didn't, then left with the threat of their return. With bigger battles to fight, they headed off, then came back, using Natchez as a base.

In my way of thinking, don't matter what your aim, no man right in his soul should commit such acts. I've always longed for a world where the word "slavery" didn't exist and planters didn't rule over the law, but if I'd known how the Yankees planned to take over, I'd have changed my prayers. Heard a Yankee say, "It'll take the fires of hell to clean the sin out of this place." But it didn't seem right cleaning sin with sin.

All I'd seen was things getting worse, not better. The planters, they still had the power over the land and the colored folks, so the only difference was that those planters had been forged in the fire of war and became bent on revenge. The anger in these parts filled the air with a heavy kind of heat that got inside you, made you ache for fresh air clean of all the pain and fear that'd bled into the soil over the years.

By the time I walked into town, my lungs ached from all that bad air. I just wanted to find me a Yankee bidder and be done with it. But on the Mississippi, the yellow fever's kin to the plague, so folks got mighty skittish when they seen me coming. Sidestepping, they moved to the boardwalk or headed into a business, anything to keep from sharing the air I breathed. With so many folks in town for the auction, I looked like a plow pushing through a field a' people, the way they just stepped back and let me through.

Fine by me; let me get to where I'm headed without all their hullabaloo about my ways. People round here didn't take to my way of doing. Didn't like my silence. Nor my britches wearing. Cried sin anytime they saw me talking to a colored person regular. Said the Bible didn't abide by it. Saying things like that just kept me in the mind to avoid that book all together. In my way of seeing things, it's colored folks who are closer to calling Jesus a relative than any of us pale people. Mrs. Wynston always told me Jesus came from Africa, same as her people. Our kin came from clear over in Europe. But such ideas had people saying I'd go straight to hell. No matter, I'd be willing to go to any kind of hell where folks admitted to such things. I'd be among friends there.

With all that fussing about me, I usually kept to home. But I had business to attend to and I wasn't going to allow nobody to stop me. 'Sides, I'd worn a dress. They should be happy with that. Or choke on it for all I cared. I hated them things, all long and heavy, tripping a person up. Still, I had to look some kind of proper if any Yankee'd be bidding on my behalf. No dress would be enough for a Northern fella to trust a stranger like me, so I stood right there in the street and prayed. I needed God to show me to a Yankee who'd bid for us and stay true.

Feeling a kind word in my soul, I headed through the doors of the Emerald Supper Club. I just marched right into that place with its could-line-a-coffin curtains and puffed-up chairs.

"Stella Reid!" Mr. Markham, the owner, popped out of his chair like it'd caught fire. "What are you doing just walking in here?"

Seemed like an obvious question to me, so I didn't answer. Besides, I didn't like how that man thought he could decide who walked where. Being the supper club owner, the auctioneer, and the town banker, he had most folks in town answering to him, but of course, he answered to Richardson, so I wasn't about to let him tell me what to do.

Mr. Poston, who stood at the front of the line to sign up for a bidding number, just stared at me like he expected me to float or something.

"I'm sorry, Stuart." Mr. Markham handed an auction bidding card to Mr. Poston. "Here's your card."

The whispering in line sounded like a mess of bugs in the reeds of a swamp. Figured I'd be hearing a bullfrog any minute. A man in the dining room coughed out all deep and low. Near about had me laughing.

Mr. Poston grabbed the card then skirted around me to rush out the door. Didn't even bother to put the auction number in his pocket.

Markham just stood by his chair. "Stella Reid, you best move on out of here, your cousin Mertle is waiting on you."

My cousin Mertle had seen more winters than Jack Frost. The only thing she waited on was the guide to take her home to the Good Lord and that sure wasn't me, so I headed on into the dining room.

Place looked near about as busy as it did come ginning time. But this crowd looked war-thin. Men in suits that'd been worn and pressed until the fabric looked ready to turn to dust. Saw more than one woman trying to hide the patches in their dresses with fans and dangling purses, but they still had their noses out of joint over seeing a girl like me walk in. I'd put on that dress, and a clean one at that. More than I usually did with my britches.

Mama used to say I wore clothes until they fell off or had enough dirt packed in them to stand on their own. Boy, how I missed her. Right then she'd be holding up a glove like them ladies leaning over tables to talk about me. But Mama'd be smiling and saying things like, "You think rose petals in your tea makes your breath sweeter?"

I'd laugh, then the ladies'd stare at me like I'd cursed their mama. One of them evil ladies, a Mrs. Violet Stevenson, even came to my mama's house with one of her dog-ugly dresses, saying, "I thought I'd be neighborly and be certain that Gayle Anne had a fitting dress to be buried in."

To bury her, I'd put Mama in the dress she wore when she married Daddy. When I told her, Miss Violet acted like I'd done killed Mama myself, saying how I'd insulted the Lord. Now, what God cared about a person's death suit, I had no idea, but Miss Violet near about made enough racket to wake the dead so we could ask them.

Mrs. Wynston had to ask that crazy lady to leave.

Wonder what that lady would've done if I told her I'd been fixing to bury Mama just as I planned to be buried, wearing the suit I wore when I came into this here world. Seemed right to me, but Mrs. Wynston said Mama wouldn't take to the idea. I had to agree.

Since my ideas rarely settle right with people, I prayed that day might be different. Started spotting up Yankees. The uniforms of the officers stationed in town didn't exactly count, those fellas wouldn't be bidding on land today. They might buy a thing or two at the auction in the big room at the back of the club, but most of them be counting the days until their general say they can go home. That morning, Markham'd auction off furniture and farming implements, any old things that'd survived the war that folks could sell off for a little holding-over money, something to get them to the next harvest.

Wouldn't be till the afternoon that folks would finish off their lunches and mosey on down the creek road to Oak Grove. That's how much time I had to find me the right bidder.

The folks waiting in line and getting impatient made Mr. Markham give up on shooing me, so I went to the cash-out counter where folks paid for their bids and their meals. Mrs. Markham didn't even offer a how do. She never did like me. Then again, I wasn't one for the silly prattling on she loved so much.

"Any Yankee bidders sign up?" I asked, knowing she kept track of every bidder who came through the line.

"Pardon?"

"Yankees looking for land."

She laughed. "It's a bit late to try selling Oak Grove, isn't it? Our bank owns it already."

I hate it when people answer a question with a question. They're trying to get something they want out of the deal. I just wanted my answer. Seeing as how it didn't look like she'd give me one, I turned to look at the folks eating. Mrs. Granville had eaten her noon meal at the table by the kitchen every day since she'd sold the place after the death of her husband back when my mama was but a girl. Didn't recognize the fella by the far window, but the yellow cotton of his suit said *Southerner* as loudly as the dark brown tweed on the fella by the piano yelled *Yankee*.

I headed straight for him, praying God had picked a fella who believed in providence showing up in the person of a young girl carrying a bagful of money and a pretty good idea.

Mrs. Markham followed me, saying, "I don't serve unescorted young ladies in my restaurant, Miss Stella."

Fine by me. I didn't come to eat. I sat down across from that fella sipping his lemonade.

"Miss Reid." Mrs. Markham stood over me, waiting for me to leave.

The Yankee wiped the sweat from his forehead with his napkin, then said, "Do you serve young ladies seated with gentlemen with wallets?" He tapped his pocket.

Mrs. Markham squinted. "I suppose."

"Thank you, ma'am. Please do bring this young lady a lemonade."

Off she went and I set to laying out my plan for this fella who kept mussing with his mustache like he thought he might've gotten food stuck in it. When I finished my pitch, the man, who turned out to be one Jeffery Hines from New Hampshire, just sighed, then said, "Seems to me, young lady, that what you need is a man of good breeding who could take your hand in marriage and see to this land of yours so you can turn your attention to more feminine pursuits."

Did that man suck on a lemon? Or just eat it whole? The idea. I didn't need no husband. I needed a way to keep my land.

Mrs. Markham showed up with the lemonade and the fella went all *thank you* and such. I felt like spilling that drink on him. But even more so, I hoped I wasn't supposed to be the wife this fussy Yankee needed. *Good Lord, please don't let this man be the one.*

A. LaFaye

"It just so happens that I have a son about your age who should be marrying soon."

Son didn't sound much better to me.

"You planning on bidding on the land, then?"

"Why bid for what could be yours by rights?" He smiled, making that mustache of his bristle up. "If we had a marriage proposal to offer, we could stop this auction right now. We'll call in the family lawyers and insist on a review of the books. That bank will change its mind when our lawyers are done with them."

That Hines fella sat all stiff and proud like he'd come up with the cure for yellow fever. And I just wanted to run off before I caught something no one could cure. I did my best "Thank you, I couldn't possibly" and set off to find someone else.

Heard the *buzz, buzz* of whispers as I walked by tables, them folks in there like wasps hovering, waiting for a sting. Heard some of them talking on Miss Mertle, saying, "That old woman's gone soft in the head, giving that girl money."

"Wouldn't give that girl a dime to feed her dying mouth."

Each sting filled my heart up with more anger, pushing me to find me a bidder, prove to those trash-talking no accounts that that I could take care of my own self, thank you very much.

But the next fella I tried throwing in with told me to get along before he called for the sheriff. The fella after him just laughed and kept on laughing like I'd said the funniest thing he'd ever heard. All that laughing sent me to the farthest table, to a man who seemed more interested in the book he was reading than the meal in front of him.

I sat down. He didn't even take no notice.

"Pardon."

"Pardon what?" he asked, keeping his eyes on his book.

"Me."

He looked up, his eyes all squint and suspicion. "And just who are you?"

"Stella Reid. I'm looking for a bidder on the plantation."

He set his book down, looking all cross-legged and official-like. His clothes as ironed-out and flat as his words. "And why would you be doing that?"

"Place was my daddy's. Ain't got the will says it's mine." That Yankee didn't need to know Daddy planned to will it to us all just yet.

Besides, he cut me off there, saying, "Fathers." He shook his head like the very word put a bad taste in his mouth.

Didn't want him to think bad on my daddy, but I had no time to be pussyfooting around. "I got money here, enough to outbid the fella they figure on being top bidder today." I patted my satchel. "If'n I can find a bidder who'd be willing to give me a stake in the place. You plan on bidding?"

"I don't believe it's any of your business whether I plan to bid or not."

I made ready to say that living on the plantation in question gave me just such a right, but then I saw the bidding number tucked into his book. No need to cause a fuss if I already knew he planned on bidding. With that fact known, I had to find out what kind of planter he'd be. I wanted Oak Grove to be in good hands.

"You know a lot about plantations?"

He let out a huff of a sigh, then said, "Young lady, I don't see why you feel the need to bother me."

117

"What I need is to know if a fella like you might give me a stake in the place if I paid good money for it."

"You expect to help run a plantation?" He looked about ready to laugh.

Made me want to leave, but I said, "The folks been running the place since before I's born. They'll keep on."

"I've heard about the coloreds of Oak Grove. They say they're still living there like they don't know the war's over, while half their countrymen have moved north. Quite a productive lot too, I hear."

I hated how this man talked about the folks like they were stupid or something, but I could see the door the Lord'd opened for me. He'd been all *be on your way*, but now he'd started talking to me and I could see by the look in his eye, he had him plans for Oak Grove. This man didn't measure up to my idea of a good business partner, but there's no better guide than God, so I walked on through, figuring He could see things clearer than me.

"You figure you'd hire on those folks if you bought the place?"

"The 'folks,' as you call them, will be quite useful, but I don't see any call for a wayward young woman who belongs in the comforts of what family she has left."

Anger started building up inside me like a smithing fire, growing so hot I just wanted that man to melt away. But I couldn't even wish for such a thing. Not if he planned on keeping the folks to Oak Grove. That is, if he aimed to treat them regular and didn't plan on sharecropping.

"You mean to lease land to them?"

He seemed a touch confused, like I'd asked him something he

didn't understand. "My business affairs are none of your concern, Miss Reid."

With his steel jaw and sharp tongue, I couldn't see what this man needed. Yet, I had to know if he planned on doing right by the folks of Oak Grove or I'd have to find me another bidder. "I've got money here. Money to see to it Daniel Richardson don't get his hands on the place."

"What you have is an ill understanding of how the world works, Miss Reid. And you best put yourself under the wing of someone who can teach you."

Why couldn't he just choke on that food he'd ordered?

The anger took a hold on me, yanked me out of my chair and had me yelling, "I want to know what you have planned for Oak Grove!"

"You'll quickly find that the world will give little regard for what you want, Miss Reid." He opened his mouth to say something else, but my heart had had its fill of bitterness.

I stormed right out of that place like he'd set a fire in me and I had to head to water to put it out. Why'd God send me into that club if all He meant to do was show me what a fool I'd been?

Wasting all that time trying to find a bidder with nothing to show for it but a soul-burning anger. Now the morning's auction would start in the back room, but I'd never go in there to find me a bidder. No, somebody'd have to kill me to make me step foot into a place where they used to sell people. Living, breathing people. I swore never to step foot in that place. And not even a threat to Oak Grove would make me break that promise.

So I walked right into the street. Saw a line of colored folks at the back of the supper club, waiting at a window. No place in town allowed colored folks to go inside to eat, and the only café to try serving food to them through the back door got shut down by the Klan, so I figured those folks be waiting in line on bidding numbers.

Saw Mr. Vinson near to the front, looking like he feared they'd try to take his money. Had to stay and watch, thinking I might could do something for him.

A fellow appeared at the window. Holding up a handful of numbers, he said, "I got me five numbers left. Who'll pay five dollars?"

Five dollars? That'd give you a bed in a hotel for a good long while. What he doing charging them money?

"Five dollars? You charging the folks inside for them numbers?" someone shouted from the back of the line.

"That makes them ten dollars. Who's got ten dollars?"

"I do!" Mr. Vinson stepped up, money in hand.

"Then this man gets him a number." He pushed the man in front aside to let Mr. Vinson approach. He started counting out change. The man laughed. "I look like a piggy bank, boy?"

He knocked the change to the ground. "Give me cash money."

"I got it, sir. It's all here. Ten dollars."

That pig for a man had Mr. Vinson on the ground, picking up the change to pay him. Weren't a bank in town that'd change money for a colored man and Mr. Vinson probably wanted his bills for the land sale.

Wanted to march up there and give that pig his money, but that was for Mr. Vinson to do.

"Next!" the man shouted.

But Mr. Vinson put his handful of coins back on the sill, saying, "It's ten dollars. Spends like any other money. I'll take my number."

"Fine!" Man threw the number out the window and it flew off over the line of men. I could see them wanting the chance to grab it, knowing they'd never make it to the front of the line. But when it fell, a young fellow, not much older than me, reached down, picked it up, then handed it to Mr. Vinson.

"Thank you, son." Mr. Vinson took that number and sighed before putting it in his pocket. The young man nodded, then turned to face the window again, still hoping for his chance.

I headed out of town after Mr. Vinson, just chewing on my own anger, trying to break it down so I could see clear of it, pray my way to seeing God's plan in all this nonsense. By the time I reached the creek road, I just felt empty. No anger. No hope. Just nothing. By failing to find me a bidder, I done left the folks of Oak Grove to Richardson, which made me no better than the low-down pig of a fella who treated Mr. Vinson so poor. *Lord forgive me.*

Auction Block

Wandered the trees, praying I'd stumble into a way out of the mess I'd gotten myself into, but the only thing I could keep in my mind but a second was what the Lord had told me, *"Find the man who needs what you have."*

What I had was nothing. Not even my own ideas.

But when I saw the people start coming down the road, I knew I had to face my mistakes, maybe find me a bidder in that crowd forming by the gin. They planned to do the auction from the storehouse. With the doors open, Mr. Markham, the banker and auctioneer, had himself a stage where he could see all the bidders down below. Also gave the people a good view of the fields and the house and all that. Just as I'd figured, people swarmed over the place like Mama's bees. Thought of breaking open her hives to really give those people something to buzz about. Smiled over the idea of all those fan-flapping, hat-turning folks running this-a-way and that-a-way, their arms a-flailing, the bees a-stinging.

But no, they just stuck their heads in doors, knocked on support posts, and went on about how Daddy might have crooked ideas, but he had him a straight transom. I'd like to straighten them out with a transom upside the head, but the Good Lord frowns on such things. Didn't stop me from thinking them though.

"What's that building for?" asked a fellow with nothing but sweat on the top of his head. He pointed to the meeting house.

"Oh, now," Richardson stepped out, fingers in his vest pockets acting like he done bought Oak Grove already. "If you'll believe it, Mr. Sebastian Reid built that eyesore to hold meetings with his coloreds."

"What for?"

Richardson laughed. "The man actually thought they should have a say in how the place was run."

"Like them darkies know the first thing about farming," said Hendersen, cleaning his teeth with a pick. "Won't a one of them do a lick of work if you don't put the screws to them."

I stepped up to have a word, but that book-loving Yankee who made me mad enough to chew glass just up and beat me to it. "Appears to me they look quite ready to bid on some good farmland."

He nodded to the folks from Oak Grove standing just beyond the gin, waiting on a chance to bid. I felt a rush of good fortune. God had done sent me a man who would stand up for the folks of Oak Grove. He weren't no Daddy, but he sure was the best I'd come across all day.

Ellis, the lawyer, came around Hendersen snarling as usual. "A bunch of uppity darkies, thinking they can bid in this here auction." He spit on the idea.

Hendersen said, "Darkies don't think! They only do what they're told."

The Yankee said, "My father always said, 'A man wed to his

ideas is as good as chained down. You, sirs, appear veritably imprisoned by your backward thoughts. Give yourself a little freedom by trying a few new ideas."

I smiled to see that stranger just square off with them small-minded men.

Ellis and Hendersen looked ready to eat that man's head, but Mr. Richardson patted the lawyer's shoulder to calm him down. "And just who gave you the idea that you could come in here and bid on land tilled by good Southern stock since before you carpetbaggers ever even thought to make this here part of your country?"

The Yankee didn't even blink; that iron way of his kept him stiff and strong in Richardson's big wind of nonsense. He made to speak, but then the shout went up to start things off.

My heart took to skipping like a rock over a pond, me trying to screw up the courage to ask that man if I could throw in with him. But I could see it in the stiffness of his shoulders, the way he walked right past Richardson's evil glare—that man wouldn't hear a word I had to say, unless . . . If'n he really was the man God had picked to help me keep Oak Grove, then he'd need something I had. But what?

All I could do was wait. Just wait and pray for God to give me the chance to get in on the bid.

"Good afternoon. Good afternoon," Mr. Markham called from his makeshift stage. "We have a fine piece of property for you today. We have two lots on the docket. A good strong piece of fallow land and the plantation proper. A nice round seventeen hundred acres sold with the full lot. Over nine hundred cleared for cotton. There's corn. There's hay. An orchard with apple, peach, and plum. Blacksmith shop. Dairy. Stables with fine quarter horse stock. Twenty in number. They have thirty head of milking cows fit for beef. Chickens, goats, and stray dogs. The house you see been standing in that spot for nearly a hundred years with its two parlors, a sitting room, verandas front and back, and four sleeping rooms. Now, there's been some fire damage to the porch, but the house is solid and in fine condition."

Fine my big toe. The big old scorch mark on the house would sure turn away a few bidders. Not to mention that pile of rubble that used to be the west porch. And wasn't that just the plan. Richardson stood there proud as a new daddy, ready to bid.

Markham shouted, "But first, we're selling off fallow land. Got two hundred seventy odd acres as prime as the fields you see here. We'll start the bidding at five dollars an acre."

"Who'll give me five?" A number went up, made my lungs seize, as I searched the crowd for Mr. Vinson. Found him on the edge of the field, looking as scared as I felt.

My mind started spinning over the numbers. That put the price at over 1,300 already and Mr. Vinson told me a week back that they only had about 1,200. Oh, Lord, let them have raised a mess more. Maybe Mr. Garrett would change his mind about his daddy's money if they needed it.

"Five and a quarter. Who'll give me five and two bits?"

Mr. Vinson's number went up.

Mr. Markham just kept calling. "Five and a quarter."

The bidding had pulled the folks of Oak Grove up close, each of them standing tight together, almost like they held each other up.

As the price climbed, Mr. Vinson kept bidding, getting closer each time to the stage, but Mr. Markham wouldn't call on him or the handful of other colored bidders.

All I could see was the hate on the faces of the folks by the gin as they watched. Not just for seeing the land they'd worked for generations slip out from under them, but for the very idea of an auction.

Selling a home's one thing, but many of the older folks had been sold themselves or watched their own kin being sold away. And the very same people who done bought the likes of them at such auctions stood right there bidding on the only place they'd called home for near their whole lives. They had every right to be hating what they saw. I would've given my life to see to it that this would be one auction that went in their favor.

At six and a quarter, Mr. Vinson shouted, "Six and a half!"

That started heads shaking. The bidders didn't like the price.

Everybody knows fallow land's in such a state 'cause it's tired out, not fit for cotton for a while. You can't get top dollar for it and your crop's bound for slim pickings, so the bid had already gone high at six.

Richardson looked ready to grind his teeth out of his mouth. He bumped a fellow who'd been bidding behind him, growling, "Bid."

"I seen that land," he snapped back. "Won't be ready for planting for five years easy. I'm not wasting my money."

Well, money had Markham finally seeing Mr. Vinson. "We have six and a half. Going once."

But did Mr. Vinson have it? I could see him fretting and figuring. Mr. Quincy there beside him talking in his ear. Mr. Lennox come running.

"Going twice."

"You got that money, boy?" Richardson yelled.

Six and a half. Six and a half. That meant they needed 1,750. Found myself inching closer in case they needed the money I held, which just kept getting heavier and heavier in my satchel.

Mr. Lennox passed off money, shoving it in Mr. Vinson's pocket.

"We have it!" Mr. Vinson shouted.

Whew.

"Sold. At six and half to Gabe down here. Boy going to see if he can farm!" Mr. Markham shouted. Others laughed.

"Dirt farming," someone whispered.

Richardson, Ellis, and them closed around Vinson, Quincy, and Lennox. Richardson shoved Mr. Vinson, "You got you cash for that, boy? No credit here!"

Mr. Vinson took a step back, then stiffened. He could see Ellis circling back with two other fellows. They meant to pick a fight. I checked the Yankee to see if he had an eye on things. He sure enough did, right out of the corner, but he kept his face front, his arms folded, like he didn't see a thing. That yellow stripe of his done run down his back 'stead of his pants.

Well, Mr. Vinson saw the writing in the dirt. He turned away, saying, "I'm going to pay my price." Richardson grabbed for his shirt, but Mr. Quincy broke through his grip, saying, "Pardon me, sir. Pardon me." Then he and Mr. Lennox shuffled Mr. Vinson off to pay up.

Richardson moved to pursue, but Markham called out, "And now for the whole of Oak Grove. Who will start the bidding at forty thousand?"

Forty? That'd clean jumped over Mr. Quincy's guess of thirty. I flashed a look to the crowd, they didn't seem one bit surprised.

That stiff Yankee lifted his chin, looking all seriouslike.

The man with the sweaty head bid forty. And with that the bidding got started, Mr. Markham calling off numbers like a deep-throated chicken, folks putting up their numbers here, then there. Even that mustache-twisting matchmaker Hines got in on things.

Each time, Mr. Richardson standing in the back, looking all cool and distracted, even chatting with his friends, waiting for Markham to repeat the bid, even letting him say, "Last call for 42.9," before he held his number up. Gloating old goat.

Could feel the eyes of the folks by the gin watching me. Felt like turning to dust myself, knowing just how I'd failed them. And Daddy.

Heard Ellis say, "See, look at them darkies just standing there. Like I said, lazy as the day is long."

I wanted to pray for the pulley over his head to come crashing down and knock some sense into him, but I had to keep praying to see the man God wanted me to see.

When the bidding hit 47.5, just two matching-suit bidders I pegged as brothers and a fella with a cut under his eye kept up with Richardson. Right before Markham upped the bid, that mean Yankee finally put his number up.

47.9, 48, 48.2. The brothers dropped out, shaking their heads and walking off.

Richardson smiled as he held up his number to bid 48.5.

48.9, 49.5, 50, 50.2, 50.3, bidding had started to slow. Markham could see the fella with the scar looking tense. 50.5.

The scar fella shook his head, then disappeared into the crowd.

Richardson smiled and held up his card.

The Yankee tensed up, his jaw looking ready to pop through the skin. Figured he'd reached his limit. And the bag in my hand suddenly felt about as heavy as a bale of cotton. *I see it, Lord. I see it.*

"50.5, going once."

I ran for him. "I got me near about three thousand."

"50.5 going twice."

"For what?" He looked startled.

"A stake in the place."

"Final call for 50.5."

He raised his eyebrows, considering it, a smile playing at the corners of his mouth. He bid, saying "50.7." Richardson looked about ready to eat that Yankee's heart whole. Then that Yankee's stiffness came back with a growling vengeance as he said, "What you'll *get* is your money back, when I have it."

That's what the man said, but I saw the Lord's hand in this here bidding as if He'd reached down from a cloud. Just like God'd said, I had the money this fella needed. God'd surely keep His promise about me living out my days on Oak Grove.

50.9, 51.2. And Richardson shifted his weight before lifting his card. Had he finally hit his limit?

Saw that the folks had moved closer, hanging on those bids like I did. Saw each one as a step, getting us closer to reaching home again, calling this place ours.

51.5. The Yankee bid. Richardson leaned over to Ellis, whispered in his ear. We'd found his limit.

"51.5 going once."

Ellis nodded.

"51.5 going twice."

Richardson put his number up. *Blast it all.*

"51.5. Who will give me 51.7?"

With his little loan, Richardson went all the way up to 53.3 without blinking.

"You have anything else?" the Yankee asked, a bit of the nerves shaking his voice. "Jewelry, china, anything?"

"A necklace."

"What's it worth?"

"No telling, but it's old."

The Yankee cursed. "I can't bid with jewelry I've never seen."

Saw Mr. Vinson lifting his chin to ask how we fared. He knew most of the folks be needing wage money and a good distance between them and Richardson. I shook my head to say we'd gone over what we could pay.

Could see the disappointment and fear passing from face to face among the folks as the word went out. They knew that if Richardson got top bid, their lives would be hard. Harder than that worn earth they'd just bought. Richardson had bid already. Second call went up.

What now? *Dear Lord, show me the way.*

"Bid," I said, hoping to buy us time.

"I'd be biting into operating money," the Yankee whispered like he might be confessing something or trying to convince himself.

Last call.

Couldn't help it. The tension of it all sent me to grabbing his arm, near about willing it to go up.

He looked down at my hand on his arm, then he followed my eyes to see the folks shoulder to shoulder and looking soul-thin.

His hand went up.

Did the man actually have a care in that cold heart of his?

53.9, 54, 54.3, 54.5, 54.7, 54.9, 55.

"The Lord will provide." I kept repeating that prayer to hold myself together.

The bidding kept going up, Richardson getting madder by the minute, shifting his weight like a bull ready to charge out of the stall, twisting his cuff as he waited for the Yankee to call his bid. Kept chatting up Ellis, but the lawyer just shook his head. Richardson had called in his last loan. He had no more money. And from the scowl on his face, I figured the Yankee must be running low his ownself.

The price hit 55.5 and I felt myself sinking into the dirt. How much more did that Yankee have?

Richardson bid.

"I can't go higher. I've spent nearly every dollar I have with me." The Yankee shook his head.

"55.5 going twice."

Please, oh please, dear Lord. He wouldn't lead us this far if he didn't mean for us to win out, so I pushed up that Yankee's hand and shouted, "56!"

A gasp went through that crowd like God'd put a crack in the sky.

The Yankee swung his arm back like I'd tried to hurt him or something. He scowled down at me. "What did you just do?"

"The necklace will be enough. It's over a hundred years old."

"So are rocks. But they're worthless."

Richardson started swearing and pacing, then yelled, "Verify!"

Mr. Markham looked a might worried as he asked, "Can you verify that bid, Mr. Dooley?"

So that's his name, Dooley.

He looked at me, then Markham, then the house, then back to Markham. "56."

"Mr. Richardson?"

Richardson shook his head and shook it, like he'd done been knocked on the skull.

56 once.

56 twice.

56 last call.

Sold to Mr. Conrad Dooley for fifty-six thousand dollars.

Richardson stormed over. "I'll tell you this, you carpetbagging son of a whore, you better have every dime of that money cash because Markham won't be taking no notes on this here auction."

"Seeing as how I'm new here and all, I'll kindly give you the chance to apologize to my mother. As a judge's wife, she can be a bit sensitive to that kind of talk." Dooley stepped closer, shoulders stiff, hands loose in his pockets, a fella used to squaring off with the likes of Richardson. Now that would come in right handy.

Richardson huffed. "Well, you just try to register that deed with the judge over at the county seat. Tell him his cousin Daniel sends his regards." And off went that bag of wind.

"You get that necklace and now."

"It's in town."

"Town?" He grabbed my hand and squeezed so hard, I felt it in the tips of my fingers. "If I don't have every penny, they will tar and feather me!"

That man had me so scared, I thought I'd shatter like a dropped pitcher, then Mr. Garrett came up, hat in hand, saying, "Mr. Dooley, sir."

"Yes?" Dooley looked downright frightened himself.

"My daddy run him that blacksmith shop down yonder and I'd be willing to pay you cash money for it. Or at least the equipment inside. Most of it's done up special by my daddy."

"Come again?" Mr. Dooley looked spooked.

But I knew a miracle when I seen it walking up on two feet. Mr. Garrett was making a bid to buy his daddy's shop in the only way he could. Wouldn't Mr. Beeman be proud to have his son working metal in his own forge. If they weren't just gifts from heaven, the lot of them.

Dooley looked down the row to the shop, then back at Mr. Garrett, saying, "And you have the cash?"

Mr. Garrett said, "If the price is fair."

Mr. Dooley stiffened, going right back to his tough Yankee ways like he weren't facing Richardson and his crew if he didn't come up with the full amount in another few minutes. "Well, I would say, I could let it go for fifteen hundred, that is with a contract for the plantation of course—you do all of our metal work for a fair rate."

Mr. Garrett tried to hold himself to a slight smile, but that man done glowed. "It's a deal, sir."

"Indeed." Mr. Dooley shook hard. "And you have the cash, then?"

"Right now?"

"Well, I have a rather large bill to settle." I could see Mr. Markham parting through the crowd to get to Mr. Dooley.

"But we ain't signed nothing yet."

"Well, you can certainly trust Miss Reid here, can't you?" He nodded to me.

I could feel the tight hold of a lie settling on me. I'd told Mr. Vinson I'd never make a promise, but here Mr. Dooley had me doing just that. Felt like stopping him, but with Markham closing in and Oak Grove almost in our hands, I just couldn't say a word.

"Sure do." Mr. Garrett nodded. "I'll get the money and send it with Miss Stella here to the bank."

"You do that." Mr. Dooley nodded, then turned like he didn't have a care in the world. "Why, Mr. Markham, let's just go on over to your fine bank and count out your money. It was so good of you to hold on to my funds." And just like I'd been holding onto his own suitcase for him, that Yankee done lifted my satchel out of my hands.

I just stood there stunned. Wasn't sure if I'd been delivered or fleeced. Like going to a tent meeting, feeling all full of praise and glory when the preacher's talking, then watching his faith come off like a mask when he stepped off the stage. Happened in nothing but a bit of time, but I seen it when Mama dragged me down to the river for a tent meeting. Man put the fire under folks, then stepped off the stage, his eyes holding nothing but a lie as he stepped down. A confidence man in it for the money in the collection plate.

But then I'd heard a preacher at Potter's Creek bring heaven a bit closer to earth with his fine words. That man spoke true words of Glory and gave me the feeling God'd come down for a visit.

So, watching that Yankee Dooley head on off to the bank with Mr. Markham, I weren't sure if I'd allowed myself to be fleeced by a confidence man or led by a true believer.

The Storm

Found the Beemans in their shop when I got back from the bank. Couldn't stop thanking them. Hugging the boys and shaking Mr. Garrett's hand. His daddy, our beloved Mr. Beeman, would've been right proud of him that day. But it did seem a shame for him to be buying what should've belonged to his daddy in the first place.

Hattie, Miss Maggie, and Mr. Vinson came on by to congratulate them on owning their very own business. I could see Mr. Quincy and Mr. Lennox coming along too, with a whole crowd of folks walking down the road to celebrate all we'd done kept and claimed as our own. Well, I'd kept Oak Grove from Richardson. The Beemans bought their family shop. And the folks had them a good piece a' land.

Still and all, I felt like flying. Seeing Hattie, I said, "We got it. We got it. It's ours!" The words just kept a-flowing like water from my mouth. Hattie took my hands and we set to jumping for joy.

Mr. Vinson put his hand on my shoulder, to quiet me down, saying, "Now, Miss Stella, you don't own the place no more. You just kept it from going to Richardson. That's a good thing, but Oak Grove ain't yours no more."

Felt like he done cut my wings clean off. Had me wanting to defend myself, saying, "Well, you can tell the folks who couldn't go in on the land that Dooley said he'd hire you all on." He didn't say that exactly, but that's what I took him to mean when he said all he did on the folks being useful and such.

"You got that in writing?" asked Mr. Vinson.

Never even thought of it. "I got it from the Lord."

Ripping his hat off his head, Mr. Quincy shouted, "Y'all got a sickness if you think that man going to honor that there agreement!" I knew for true that he meant to save his house, which stood on Oak Grove proper.

"Hush now!" Mr. Vinson barked. Taking my hands in his, he said, "Now, Miss Stella, you think you can get me a meeting with this here fella, so we can iron this all out regular?"

"Sure." But I didn't feel so sure as I watched Quincy and them spread the news. All those looks of ten kinds of happy I'd just seen melted right down to worry and fear, back where they'd been when the auction started.

"But God sent me to Dooley," I told Hattie.

"That don't mean Dooley answers to God," Hattie said back.

I looked at Mr. Vinson. He nodded. "Don't agree to no thing you ain't got in writing."

What had I done?

Felt like I'd been pulled up into a twister. All those people crossing this-a-way and that-a-way as they fretted over what Dooley might do tore me up inside. Why, I'd made the biggest mistake of not just my life, but the life of every person who ever planted a seed on Oak Grove.

About ready to bury myself into the ground, I headed off to clear my head, find a way out of that storm I'd thrown us into. Back at the office, I leaned on the door to let the wave of all that fear and anger and worry just wash over me, but another one came right behind it. Had me crying and shaking.

"Stella?"

I turned to see Hattie standing there. With my back to the door, I slid down to the ground.

"You figured a man you never done meet before in your life going to buy this place for all of y'all. Just like that?"

"No." I tried to pull in all that storm and strife, just push it back down inside me. "God showed him to me."

Either that or I'd taken a greedy man's need for more money as a sign. "Or I thought He did."

Hattie sat beside me. "Then we just gonna sit right here and pray you was right." Taking my hand, she nodded, then set to praying.

But my heart had gone all stiff, holding in all the words of prayer.

I had to ask her, "You think he gonna send us off?"

"Might could."

Just those two words cracked the lid I'd put on all those nasty feelings. Had me sobbing all over again.

Hattie just hugged me and rocked.

Dooley came from the stables and walked right on by us like we were nothing more than possums under a bush. He went inside the house and did something I hadn't seen or heard anyone do in all my days. He locked the door.

I never did claim that house as my own, but being denied a

way in felt wrong down to my bones. Had me thinking that Dooley would find him a way to get me off Oak Grove permanent.

Wasn't long before I heard the bell ringing to call a meeting. Folks would be talking this all out and I had to speak for my actions.

I got up. Hattie didn't let go of my hand. Seemed fine by me. What with me waiting to see what Dooley would do and her waiting on what might happen with her folks up at that Adams County Courthouse, seemed pretty right for us to stay together.

Walking into that meeting house felt like I'd taken a wrong turn and ended up in one of Mama's hives, the place all bustling and buzzing with anger. Seeing me, folks took to snarling and talking real low and quick.

Didn't even bother sitting, knew I'd worn out my welcome. Hattie stood right beside me just a-holding my hand.

"All right. All right." Mr. Vinson waved to have folks settle down. "Let's start things off."

"What was you thinking, Miss Stella?" asked Mr. Lennox.

Miss Maggie shot up from her chair, shouting, "Andrew Jackson Lennox, ain't nothing more important than prayer. You shut your mouth till the pastor's done thanking the Good Lord for the land we did get."

Mr. Lennox backed up as Mr. Vinson nodded to the pastor. "Father Rallsom."

He hadn't even finished the "amen" before Mr. Lennox yelled, "What says that Yankee's any better than Richardson?"

My heart just shrank up into nothing more than an empty peanut shell. How right he was. Where had my mind been?

On doing the right thing. But what right did I have to go

trusting a man just 'cause he defended the folks of Oak Grove and said he'd give them work? And that's all he did was say it. Weren't no guarantee he'd come through on it. And then there was the matter of that promise he made on my name. Said Mr. Garrett would own the blacksmith shop. He wouldn't go back on that, would he?

Hattie whispered to me, "That Lennox's just wind, Miss Stella. Just a big old gust a' wind."

But that wind had a storm in it as Mr. Lennox said, "Just like your daddy, saying one thing, doing another."

"That's enough!" Mr. Zachariah, the stablemaster, stood up to hush him.

"What we have," Mr. Vinson spoke real loud, "is two hundred and seventy acres to call our own. We raise cotton for cash on that land and work this here place for a wage till we can buy more land. Come tax collecting, they'll be plenty a' land to be had."

"That's a plan!" shouted Mr. Jasper.

Mr. Quincy yelled, "And what says this Dooley ain't going to break this place up for sharecropping, charging us twice the worth for seed and plows and such?"

I ran through our conversation fast as I could, but then I realized Mr. Dooley never did say he wouldn't do that very same thing. He only said the folks of Oak Grove would be useful, but he never did say how. *Oh, Lord, what had I done?*

Trusted in Me.

Heard it plain and simple. And the folks around me had to know that's why I'd done what I did, so I yelled, "I prayed, then did what the Lord showed me."

You'd a thought I'd said the Lord planned to stop by for a visit the way folks turned and stared at me.

I gripped Mrs. Wynston's chair just about as hard as Hattie squeezed my hand.

Mrs. Wynston asked, "What sign you see that say it was the Lord?"

"Lord said to find the man that needed what I had. Knew He wasn't talking about Richardson, so I give the money to the only other fella still bidding."

Hattie looked shocked as she asked, "He did?"

"That a true tell?" asked Mr. Jasper.

I nodded.

He looked to Mr. Vinson. "What you think?"

"No telling without meeting this fella."

"Where is he, then?"

Hattie said, "Locked himself in the house."

I cringed to see what thunder that'd set loose.

Folks just looked sad, like they'd seen a sign of their own and didn't like what it told them.

"Dooley say what he planned for the place?" Mr. Harris asked, probably wondering if there'd be a way for him to own his woodworking shop like Mr. Garrett owned the smithy.

I shook my head.

That sent folks to grumbling.

"Well," Mr. Lennox stood, saying, "I'm not waiting here to find out. I'm heading north while the heading's good."

"I'm ready." Young Mr. Carter got up, his satchel in hand.

"Who's going?" Lennox asked. Hattie moved closer to me, like she thought they might stampede out of there and trample us.

Some folks stood up right quick, others looked from one neighbor to another, trying to decide, a few standing real unsurelike, others staying put. I tried to tell myself it weren't just the folks who'd paid in on the land who planned to stay, but that might have been a fool's hope.

"Now hold up!" Mr. Vinson moved to the center of the room. "When Mr. Sebastian say he going to build this here meeting hall, you believe him?"

More grumbling and plenty of blank stares.

"Well, did you?"

"No, sir," said Mr. Taylor, rubbing his beard.

"And what he do?"

"Built it," shouted Mr. Clark from the far corner.

"And when he say he going to give us our Saturdays *and* our Sundays off, did you believe him?"

"No, sir," shouted Mrs. Wynston's Mary Ellen.

"Then he started writing free papers. And buying folks here." Mrs. Wynston added. "You seen any other white man do that?"

"Not round here!" shouted Mr. Jasper.

"That's right. Mr. Sebastian, he done give us all he said he would," Mr. Vinson said.

"No, he didn't!" Mr. Lennox yelled so loud I felt it in my belly.

"Now, you hush about that!" Mr. Vinson stepped over, looking mean as a bear and twice as ornery. Face-to-face, those two men looked ready to throw down. "Mr. Sebastian died 'fore he could sign that deed you been going on about. That man bleed his last for the likes of you and you better start respecting him or I'll be walking you off this place my own self and you won't be coming back." As Mr. Vinson talked, Mr. Lennox just shrunk under the weight of it all. Wished I had it in me to do such a thing to that Richardson.

Folks gave Mr. Vinson a round of "That's right."

And Mr. Lennox just sat himself down.

"Now," Mr. Vinson turned to the others, saying, "Mr. Sebastian done pass his heart down to his daughter. I seen it in her face. If she say this man Dooley going to do right by us, he going to do right."

Had me feeling all funny like pride done run into fear and mixed all together, making me jittery inside. Hattie gave me a hug like she agreed with Mr. Vinson, but a part of Daddy being in me didn't sound right after what I'd done. He had too much good in him, but I never did a thing near as special as Daddy done all his life—buying folks to their families, building the meeting hall to give folks the vote, sending money to the Yankees. No, all I did was try to keep Daddy's dream moving and breathing. Wasn't doing that good at even that small of a job.

"What say you?" Mr. Vinson asked, looking out over that crowd of faces looking as confused as I felt.

"Yea," whispered Mr. Zachariah.

"Yea," said Mr. Wynston, sounded pretty sure of himself. Mrs. Wynston nodded, so did her Mary Ellen.

Mr. Jasper slapped the arm of his chair. "Darn tooting!"

Folks laughed and the yeas started pouring like rain. Hattie shouting right along with them. Soon folks turned to Lennox and his lot leaning on the back wall. Lennox didn't even look up. But Mr. Carter shrugged. "All right."

"Mr. Quincy." Mr. Vinson said his name with the soft kind of force that said *respect*.

"I'll give it till sundown tomorrow. Then I'm gone."

"Fair enough." I could see Mr. Vinson sigh, feeling a little of the tension seep out of the room. "We stay. Come sundown we see where we at and vote again."

Folks nodded.

"Meetings always like this?" Hattie asked.

Not hardly.

"Well, I'm coming to more of these." She smiled like she'd been given a pass to go to town. "It's like a revival or something."

I smiled to see her so full of energy. I just hoped her parents came back with good news. More than that, I prayed that Dooley fella had good things to tell the folks come next meeting or I'd be seeing all of my daddy's dreams just fold up like an old flower and die.

Mr. Vinson came over to me with a look that cut clean into my bones. He had that suddenly tired, kind of scared look that confidence man had when he stepped off the stage after preaching a lie. Mr. Vinson done talked up my daddy to keep people from leaving, but he didn't believe in me no more than Mr. Lennox did. Heard it in the weakness of his voice when he asked, "Miss Stella, you bring Mr. Dooley down for a vote?"

I stood. "Yes, sir."

"Good." He wrung his hands as he left.

The storm I'd brought to Oak Grove passed over it, drifting off toward the gulf as folks set to talking and planning and wondering just what that Mr. Dooley might do. All of us worried that a bigger storm might be just over the horizon waiting to strike us down.

Doomed

Like Hattie, I couldn't sleep. So we used our old route for getting into the house after dark—going in through the dining room window Daddy never fixed, then up the back stairs Mrs. Wynston always used, we slipped in real quiet.

Near about felt like days of old with us sneaking in, then having us a sit-down in the hall upstairs, a pile of peanuts between us, just cracking shells, popping nuts, and talking like we ain't got a care in the world. Of course, Hattie did the talking. I did the eating.

"Now, what I'd like to know . . ." Hattie put a hitch in that question to flick a peanut at my mouth, but she hit me in the cheek. That girl had lousy aim. Floor looked like an elephant's lunch, all strewn with peanuts she done tried to get in my mouth. "I'd like to know just what Jesus looked like. Weren't no white man. Couldn't a been. Could He?"

Cracked a peanut, knowing she had her own answer.

"Not born in the heat of Israel he wasn't. I've seen pictures of them folks in the travel books Miss Dory done keep. Those folks is near about as dark as the pale side of my arm. Jesus was a dark man. Had to be or them apostles would be talking about his pale skin, don't you think?"

Flick. She hit me in the eye. *Why did I even let her try?*

"Jesus be no taller'n me."

"What?"

"He'd be short."

"How you know that?"

I'd read a book about graveyards and coffins from way on back. Weren't no one much taller than me back then, 'lessen they cut folks off at the ankles or something to put them in the ground. "Read it."

"You can read?"

I pitched a peanut and hit her in the forehead.

She grabbed it and tossed it back. She and I had learned to read together with Mama, sitting in the very room where Mr. Dooley slept. Mama sitting on one side of the table, Hattie and I shoulder-to-shoulder on the other, our fingers side-by-side, going over them words. Her saying them out loud, me reading them in my head.

"Read the words, Stella." Mama looked all sour-faced. "Read them."

I am, I thought. And I was, but she thought I didn't read them on account of the fact I didn't say them out loud. Had her so frustrated, she'd get up and pace, her hand on her back like it hurt her.

Hattie'd read out a sentence like it meant I learned it too.

"Thank you, Hattie." Mama'd force a smile, then say, "But I need to know Stella can read it." She'd look all sad at me.

"I can."

"Can you?"

I'd nod.

She'd said, "Show me."

I'd run my hand down the page, read the whole thing, then turned the book to show her I'd done it. That usually sent her stomping out of the room, sounding like she just woke up the hive inside her mouth.

Then one day, she came over to kneel by me. "Stella, I don't know if you're reading that or just running your hand over it. Please, read it to your mama. Please."

She looked ready to cry. And if she cried it'd hurt my heart, so I took a big breath, then read me a page. No stopping. No stumbling. Just reading.

Mama laughed and clapped. Hattie just sat back and stared.

"My heavens. What more you got locked away in that head of yours?" Mama hugged me.

I put my arms around myself to remember that warm feeling and the smell of elder flower talc dizzying up my head. *Mama, I miss you till my skin aches.*

"I miss her too." Hattie tapped my knee with her foot.

We smiled, then set back to eating and talking. Hattie asked, "Wonder if Jesus had a beard that grew real long or just a short one? Did fellas shave atall back then?" And on she went until sleep robbed us of our wits.

"Miss Reid!" Mr. Dooley's shout had me up and standing like a colonel done broke into the house and made me a private.

"Yes, sir?"

"Is this any way for a young woman to act? Bringing strange

people into my home and treating it no better than a barn?" He kicked at the shells on the floor.

"We'll clean it up," Hattie said, scrambling to her feet.

"Oh, and just who are you?" Couldn't tell if the look on his face might be fear or just twisted-up, ugly anger.

"Hattie. I'm from the Hendersen place."

"Then what are you doing here?"

"She's my friend," I said.

"I can see that, but hasn't she a job to get to?" I could see the confusion just growing on his face, like he'd walked into a place he didn't understand atall.

"Hot jam!" Hattie caught sight of the sun and went a-running. "Sorry, sir, but I'm late."

I had to hold my breath to keep from laughing. The ugly look on Dooley's face helped quite a bit. "I'll get to cleaning."

"When you're done with this mess, you can turn your hand to airing this place out. It smells like an attic in here."

"Yes, sir."

Was that his plan? Turn me into his maid? That idea had revenge written all over it. Putting me to work cleaning house would only lead to his pain. I'm no good at mopping and such. Just not one to see dirt in that sort of way. I'm much better with a hoe in my hand.

After I swept the hallway, I met Mrs. Wynston on my way down to get the mop. She already had it and a bucket. "Go on, Miss Stella. I heard all that. Place be aired out by noon meal."

With a kiss to her cheek, I said, "Thank you."

"Don't you worry. It's all about not having to clean up after *your* cleaning."

I ran off laughing. But before I tried my hand at talking to Mr. Dooley again, I had to clean up and look right, so I had me a scrub in the creek, and a hair combing, then I put on the clothes I kept for services down at the creek. Looking fit, I headed down to Daddy's office for another try at that darn safe. If I could just get it open and find that will, I'd be rid of that Dooley. He couldn't own what the bank had no right to sell.

Facing the safe, I couldn't think of much except holidays Daddy really loved, like the Christmas I learned to ride the pony he bought me. We spent the whole day in that little paddock off the old stables until I kept my seat and got my reign signals right. 12-25-59. Nothing. The Easter we brought a sick calf back to full life, it getting up on its wobbling legs just as the sun rose on Easter morning. Daddy and I putting our hands up to the Lord in thanks. 4-21-62. As tight and closed as the vault in a bank.

I had no more time to dally, so I walked right up to the door that'd been put up by a Reid and used by a Reid for four generations, and I knocked.

Mrs. Wynston answered the door. "Here to see Mr. Dooley?"

I could tell by the thinning of her eyes that Mrs. Wynston didn't take to this change in things; she'd run that house for more days than I'd been alive and didn't take to having nobody tell how it's done. And Mr. Dooley struck me as a man with particular ideas. She stepped back and said what she did to every guest. "Please have a seat in the sitting room. I'll go tell Mr. Dooley you here."

Off she went.

I sat in the sitting room I rarely stepped a foot in. Kept

remembering that awful Miss Katherine Shaw and that dreadful Mrs. Stevenson. The longer I sat there, the more I realized how much I hated that room with its furry wallpaper, fancy chairs, and shiny curtains. Even with the windows full open, I felt all closed in, so I just had to leave.

Had to find that Dooley. But he wasn't in the house. Found Mrs. Wynston scrubbing the dining room floor. Couldn't quite tell if she be sweating or crying or both.

Sitting up on her knees, she said, "I'm gonna tell you, Miss Stella. That man is about to get him some root in his tea. Man told me to make you wait. I told him I didn't 'preciate him treating you bad, but he said he wouldn't stand for no servant that didn't do his bidding. Well, he better not be bidding me to make him no tea."

That man had numbered his days like a calendar if he thought he could just order Mrs. Casadine Wynston around. Right about then, finding Dooley might mean protecting him. "Where he at?"

She nodded toward the back door. That said office to me.

Now, he could lock me out of that stuffy old house, but he couldn't keep me out of my daddy's office.

I marched right up there, gave that doorknob a turn, but found it locked. Could see that stern old rock of a man sitting at my daddy's desk like he'd owned it all his life. I marched right around, popped open the window and stepped inside.

He stood up. "Young lady, you must start respecting the rules of proper decorum."

De-what? I swear that man done spoke a form of English I'd never heard tell of.

He shook his head like worry done settled into it and he had a mind to get it out. "If you don't change your ways, you'll be packed off to your relative faster than you can whistle Dixie."

I didn't even know how to whistle and I didn't care to learn. What I wanted was the log book under his hands. Nobody but a Reid had a right to write in that book.

"This place belonged to my daddy."

"It hardly belongs to him now."

"There's the kind of ownership that comes with money, then there's the kind that comes from building and working a place till you die. By them rights, this place will always be my daddy's."

Dooley looked kind of weighted down by that idea. "Then it's quite unfortunate that the law doesn't agree with you."

"I gave you the money you needed, so I could have a stake in Oak Grove. You call cleaning up after you a stake?"

"I call this a case of upbringing without a trace of proper discipline." Before I could so much as turn to leave, he had me by the collar and dragged me into the house. I fought with all I had, but he didn't so much as loosen his grip. Threw me into the china closet, then he said, "A young lady with no respect for her elders is sure to find herself shunned. To see what I mean, you can spend the rest of your day in solitude." He shut that door and locked it. "You'll come out when you've learned to behave yourself."

Had me so stunned my muscles had forgotten how to move. Stared at that door, hearing my mama say, "It's just not natural."

She'd been right all along. My odd ways had landed me in a china closet with no way out. And my head seemed like just as tight a trap. Couldn't get my mind around what to do next. Never had to deal with a fella like that Dooley before. Didn't know how to work with him. Seemed like I'd have to act like all them other girls in dresses and turned-down eyes, all "yes, sir"—"no, sir" proper. That'd kill me as sure as a shovel to the head.

Dooley Goes to Meeting

Seemed like I'd put the whole lot of us in prison. A man who could lock me in a china closet would not be a proper planter by my way of thinking. A planter had to have the good of all the people on the plantation in mind as well as his crop if he wanted to keep things moving smooth and productive-like.

But that Dooley had him an iron-tight love of the rules, the kind of foolish rules the world made up. He'd be changing every darn thing he didn't like, and by the looks of him that'd be plenty. Wouldn't be long before Lennox and his lot had everyone leaving.

I had half a mind to break out of that china closet and hit the road myself, but I couldn't look at all them pretty plates and not think on Mama—how she sat me down on her bed one day and tried to explain things to me.

"Now, Stella, I know how you love Oak Grove." She set to combing my hair. "And, at times, I do as well. But you have to realize, the way things are here isn't the way of the world."

What did I want with any silly old world that wasn't a stitch like home?

"You may not want to leave Oak Grove, but there's no telling what changes will come. Changes that would mean you'd have to leave."

I turned to ask what kind of changes those could be. Nearly pulled the hair out of my head doing it, but I had to know what could take me from the only place I called home.

Mama turned my head back to face away from her and kept brushing. "Marriage, for one, Stella. You may marry a man who owns his own land. You'll go to live on that land."

I shook my head to say I'd never do such a thing, but she stilled me with her hands over my ears. "Never say never, Stella. That tempts the devil.

"Now, I want you to listen to me. Hear what I'm telling you. Away from Oak Grove, things are different. Young ladies don't work the fields or climb on roofs. They see to the affairs of the house, raise their children, tend their gardens. Gentle, loving things." She stroked my hair, showing me just what she meant.

Then as now, I cursed myself for being born a gosh-darn girl. I loved my mama down to the last hair on her head, but I never did want to become her. I had my eyes set on following in Daddy's footsteps. The way he went outside every single day to get things done—fixing fences, staking new trees, birthing calves, training horses, talking crops with Mr. Vinson—all that went into keeping Oak Grove on the grow. That's what I wanted to do, but Mr. Dooley seemed dead set on making my mama's words come true.

Hated the idea so much my stomach soured right up, but I promised myself I'd give it a try if it'd make things run smooth for the folks of Oak Grove. I couldn't hardly help them locked in no china closet. So, I stood right up and knocked on that door, the only way I knew to show Dooley I planned to play by his rules.

Heard Mrs. Wynston say, "You better not be breaking plates, Miss Stella." When I didn't answer, she said, "I'll go find me the Iron Man." Her footsteps headed to the back door. She had a good name for him there. Fella had to be made of iron to be so stiff and proper.

I waited. No sound. Just empty air. That black-hearted fella made me wait in that room for what felt like a thousand years before he came to open it.

Stood in the hallway facing the front door like he waited for something. I recognized that look. He wanted to hear me apologize.

"I'm sorry."

He sighed, all tired-looking. "Those are empty words, Miss Reid. Tell me what you're sorry for."

For disrespecting him of course, but if you asked me, he was the one doing the disrespecting, refusing to accept me as I am, trying to make me into something I can't stand. He should've been apologizing to me.

"Miss Reid?"

He could wait until the roof rotted and fell on his head for all I cared, but I said, "I apologize for not respecting you."

"Very good. Now please, go to your room and put on some proper clothing."

If my clothes were fit enough for the Lord they should've been fit enough for the likes of him, but I went upstairs just the same. Didn't do me no good. I hadn't worn any of them clothes in years. Didn't a one of them dresses fit me.

"Miss Reid." I heard Mr. Dooley speak to me from the hall. "Are you coming out of there or not?"

"Not."

A pause that seemed filled with the steam of anger. "And why not?"

I opened the door. "Nothing fits."

"You mean to tell me, you always wear britches?" His voice had the sound of startlement in it.

"For years."

He looked as shocked as if I said I used the Lord's name in vain. "Pardon me for being crass, but how long has it been since your mother passed on?"

Not sure what Mama's death had to do with my clothes, but I said, "About two weeks."

"And she let you wear such things?"

That seemed pretty obvious to me.

"When a person asks you a question, it's polite to answer."

"Yes, sir."

"Well, I'm not about to allow a young lady under my care to be traipsing around like some dirty farmhand. First thing tomorrow, I'll take you into town for proper clothing."

Think of the folks, Stella. Think of the folks. If it weren't for them, I'd have told Mr. Dooley he could bury that "proper" of his under a thornbush, but I just nodded my head and said, "Yes, sir."

Town and proper talk, put me to thinking on Cousin Mertle. "Miss Mertle, Mertle Seeton, my mama's cousin, she be wanting to talk to you about my education and such."

"And you certainly need it with grammar like that. We'll have to stop in and see Miss Seeton."

155

"She's a Mrs."

"You said, 'miss.'"

For being so proper and high on his grammar, he didn't know much about the Southern way of saying things. When you're talking about a woman older than you, you say "Miss" and her calling name. When you're talking about a family name, you say "Mrs." So much for grammar.

"Well, Miss or Mrs., she'll have to wait until tomorrow to speak with us. For now, you can pack away your parents' things. Keep what you want in the attic."

Seeing the setting sun cast its red cape over the floor, I said, "But it's meeting time."

"I beg your pardon?"

"It's meeting time. Come sundown the folks all gather at the meeting house, so we can talk out the day. Plan tomorrow."

He blinked like I'd given him a figuring problem he couldn't solve. "Do you mean to say that the people on this plantation really do vote on how things are run?"

"Yes, sir."

He stared off a second to let that settle in. "My goodness. I've purchased Fruitlands."

A smile actually took a hold on his lips. Well, what a wonder. He could smile, but that didn't mean he made any sense. I mean, sure we had an orchard, but not enough to call it a fruit land. "Pardon?"

"Fruitlands. A community farm run by Bronson Alcott and Charles Lane. Everyone shared the work and the profit. Too bad there wasn't any profit to share." He shrugged.

"Oak Grove produces ten bales to every seven from any other place."

"Does it now?" He nodded, a touch impressed.

"Best cotton-growing land you'll ever find."

"Well, I'll just have to hear more about that. So does this meeting take place in that building they pointed out at the auction?"

Now if I told him, he'd try to make me stay behind, and I promised I'd bring him, so I said, "I'll show you."

He shook a finger at me. "Don't think I can't see the game you're playing at, Miss Reid. I know you're only angling to go yourself, but since I need an introduction, I'll agree to let you guide me. I've been waiting all day to meet the overseer of this darn place and haven't had a single person give me so much as a salutation. Except that house servant."

Who could imagine why that would happen? What with his sunny face and friendly ways, people should just be flocking to him, shouldn't they? Not if they knew what was good for them. Folks probably left him alone 'cause they expected him to make the first move. But that didn't matter now. He'd be meeting everyone in no time atall.

"That servant's Mrs. Casadine Wynston." A woman he had better respect or he could kiss his sound bowels good-bye.

"I see." He nodded, following me out the door.

The meeting hall sounded graveyard-quiet when we came up. As we walked in, the folks stopped whispering and turned to us.

Mr. Vinson stepped up to shake his hand. "Good evening, Mr. Dooley. I'm Vinson, Gabriel Vinson, the foreman."

"You mean an overseer?" Dooley stood and offered him his hand.

Mr. Vinson shook it real surelike. "I mean foreman. At Oak Grove we do things in a certain way."

"I've noticed." He looked around at all the staring faces, even seemed to share a touch of their fear. "And I hope to be brought up to speed on the place, so we can make the proper changes to maximize our efficiency."

That man sure did love proper things, but he didn't even talk regular. *"Max-a-hooey," "effic-a-whatsie," what did those funny kind of words mean?*

"That'd be right fine," said Mr. Vinson, but I could see the confusion in his eyes. He didn't know what that man said any more than I did.

Dooley turned to the group, saying, "Good evening, all. The name is Dooley, Conrad Dooley. You may call me Mr. Dooley, if you wish."

I would've liked it if his mama called him on home and he left the place to us, but that wouldn't be coming to pass anytime soon.

"Since we're not well acquainted with one another, I thought it best if we talk about our expectations. What I expect of you and what you can expect of me. Sound like a good approach?"

Folks just stared, probably putting the figure on the fella, waiting for him to say something that made good sense. Or any sense atall with his peculiar words and such.

But he just kept on going, like he might be on a stump, speechifying. "I've done a good deal of research into the plantation system. From my calculations, I believe we can ensure our success by following a few simple rules. Each morning, roll will be taken at dawn. Then it's to the fields. You can have a half an hour for lunch. We stop for the dinner meal at sundown. Children below the age of seven shall be schooled. The elderly are the responsibility of their kin. I can't be paying out for people who are no longer productive and expect to increase our profits."

Folks stared back at him, looking as empty and confused as I felt.

"Of course, you'll have the Lord's day to rest. Does this building serve as your church?"

Mr. Vinson said, "Sounds like you got our duties just so, Mr. Dooley, but what you offering us?"

"Yes, of course. Well, I've been comparing payment methods and I believe it would be quite fair to offer everyone a salary to be paid at the end of each month. Sixteen dollars for the men. Eight for the women. Six for the children under sixteen. I will provide the seed, the tools, the wagons, everything you'll need in the fields. For a small fee, of course. That also applies to the upkeep of your homes, but you'll be responsible for your own food and clothes. And I've heard a good deal about all the efforts among freedmen to build schools. I applaud that effort myself and would be glad to hire on a teacher for the children and any adults who'd care to learn to read after working hours."

"We know how to read," Mrs. Wynston said in a low, *how-dare-you* kind of voice. "And we have our own teacher, Miss Maggie."

Mr. Dooley turned right quick, looking all shocked. "You do?"

"That's right." Mr. Quincy stood up and pushed his hat back. "We can read. We can write. We can also run this plantation. We been doing it for years now."

Mr. Lennox and a few of the other folks from Mr. Quincy's

field crew backed him up with a "that's right," while others kept to their seats, whispering about wages and "watch your mouth," sounding half-hopeful, half-scared.

"I'm sure you have, Mr. . . ?"

"Quincy. Name's Quincy."

"Well, Mr. Quincy, I'm sure you've all done a fine job of running the place, but there's always room for improvement. For instance, I was hoping to hire a college-trained teacher. Someone with the education and the experience for the job."

"Uh-huh." Mr. Quincy sounded about as convinced as a bull that's been told he can fly.

And Miss Maggie looked about ready to send Mr. Dooley flying for talking down about her teaching.

But Dooley didn't pay no mind to them. He just kept right on flapping at the mouth. "That's right. I've taken on this property to make it the best plantation in the Natchez district."

Mrs. Wynston leaned in to ask me, "He know we close to that now?"

"Are we agreed on the terms, then?" Mr. Dooley looked around, smiling like he'd offered them a plantation of their own, not the worst terms they'd heard since Big Daddy ran the place. Then again, Dooley offered them money. A salary near as fair as Daddy's. Now, that might just be enough to make his plan worthwhile. That is, if they wanted to save enough to buy the land that came up for sale come tax time. Of course that'd take them clean away from Oak Grove altogether. And from the nodding I saw there were plenty of folks who took to that idea right off.

"Pardon, Mr. Dooley, you said something about fees. Can you tell us more?" Mr. Vinson asked.

"Fees?" Mr. Dooley pretended to be surprised, but I could

see a bashful kind of knowing in his eyes. "Well, I can't just offer you everything for free, so there'll be a small equipment charge, a rental fee, and a school tax."

"School tax?"

"He say rental fee?"

"Equipment what?"

The questions went up like hoes when a storm's coming in, everyone anxious and wanting to know just what he meant by all of that and how much it'd cost.

"Now, now. Let me explain." Mr. Dooley put his hands up to calm folks. "The equipment charge will help me keep everything in working order. And I'll only be charging you a nickel a day per worker. For a bed in the bunkhouse, you'll pay a mere four dollars a month. For the upkeep of the cabins, there will be a modest charge of $10.00 a month, a mere steal for such fine cabins as those. Why, I haven't seen brick cabins with windows and wooden floors on any of the plantations I've visited. As for the school tax, it's a mere fifty cents a month per student to help pay for the teacher's salary."

That little speech set a fire of anger in the place. Mr. Lennox's friend Carter spoke up right quick, asking, "And just how much work you do on those plantations you visited?"

"What I want to know," Mr. Quincy said, standing up, "is why you even bother paying us? At the rates you talking, you only paying me about $2.50 a week. And you got me paying for a house I built with material I paid for my ownself."

"You did?" Dooley asked, looking like it done surprised him that a colored man could build a house, but I know a colored man could do anything a white man could.

"That's right."

"Did each of you pay for the quarters here?"

Folks shook their heads.

"But we have land of our own," shouted Mr. Taylor.

Mr. Jasper added, "That's right, some of us got land of our own. We be building up there."

"I see. Well, then there'd be no housing charges for those with homes of their own." Mr. Dooley nodded, but looked a bit nervous. Probably didn't figure on having to pay out so much in salary. Sounded like most of the planters around here. They charged so much for this and that, sharecroppers didn't have no cash money coming to them by harvest. They owed money instead. Evil system, really. I prayed Dooley had better plans than that. Otherwise I'd be doing a lot more than putting roots in his tea.

"So, as you can see, I'm willing to pay a generous wage when most planters are only paying in cotton."

If that.

Mrs. Bishop pulled at my sleeve, asking, "How much we'd be making?"

That put a question in my head that Mrs. Wynston shouted out, "What about folks not working the fields? Cooks and maids and such."

"Now, there," Mr. Dooley nodded, looking all thoughtful and such, saying, "I must say in fairness to the others, I see no reason to offer a better wage. But," he held up a finger, adding, "if you are a tradesman, you can sell any wares not used on this plantation."

Mr. Harris, the carpenter, stood up, asking, "You giving me

162

a chance to buy my shop? Or will you be charging me for the equipment?"

Mrs. Bishop called out, "What about food stores? Who pays for that?"

"Do I pay for my cleaning things?" asked Mrs. Wynston.

And the questions started flying around like locusts.

"Hold now," pleaded Mr. Dooley, but them questions just kept buzzing, so he whistled loud enough to stop a plow horse in its tracks. "What I was going to say is that I will be sitting down with each and every person to write out a contract. A contract for the sale of the blacksmith shop." He pointed to Garrett Beeman and I felt like he done take a whole sack of horseshoes off my back. Felt good to know that promise he made on me would be made good. "And a contract for each and every person who works on this plantation so we are all clear on our duties and our salaries and a detailed account of who pays for which expenses." He looked around real slowlike, then asked, "Does that sound fair?"

Folks set to talking things over among themselves.

Mrs. Bishop asked again, "So how much that mean we be making?"

I did the math as quick as I could for two adults, four working children, a baby, and one schoolchild. "Thirteen dollars."

"A week?"

"A month." At that rate, it'd take them over a year to be able to buy a decent spread of land with no house and that's if they didn't eat nor buy new clothes.

Mr. Jasper asked, "And the doc? Who pays for the doc?"

"Why, you'd pay your own doctor bills, of course. And there's the rental fee for the church, here."

"We have our services by the creek," Mrs. Wynston said. "You going to be charging us for the use of the ground?"

"Of course not, Mrs. Wynston."

Well, at least he'd learned her name.

Mr. Zachariah said, "Mr. Reid done give us Saturday and Sunday off. Saturday give us time to work our own land."

He took in a breath, then said, "Well, I understand that, but I'm not Mr. Reid now, am I?"

Wasn't that the truest thing that man had said since I'd met him. That Dooley'd be Cain to Daddy's Abel, that's for sure. A right nasty man he was. Even had me thinking I'd done settled for a lesser evil. That Richardson couldn't have been much worse than him.

"So we're agreed, then?" Dooley still had that stupid smile on his face like he'd offered something fair.

"What if we want something different?" asked Mr. Lennox.

"Then, I'm afraid I'd have to suggest that you can look elsewhere. These are the terms for this plantation. You can take them or leave them."

"Well, I be leaving 'em."

And just like that, Mr. Lennox walked off, Mr. Carter not two steps behind. The Benson family followed. But most of the folks kept in their chairs, turning this way and that, talking to friends, neighbors, and family, trying to sort out all they'd heard.

Mr. Dooley didn't even watch Mr. Lennox and his lot leave, he just took his watch out and started to polish it.

"You gonna give us plots?" asked Mr. Yates from the east field crew.

"Not productive enough." Mr. Dooley shook his head.

"Plantation farming is far more productive than smaller plots. We'll continue to work the land gang style."

"With you owning everything?" shouted someone from the back corner.

"That's correct. As I said, you'll be contract workers. Each of you will sign a contract. Each contract states that you will work under my employ for one calendar year. Next year at this time, your work performance will be evaluated. If your work is satisfactory, then you'll be offered a new contract."

Did this man hunt for words we couldn't understand? Now, I'd heard of contracts from land contracts, but eval-*what?* And I'd heard tell of "satisfactory" before—Hattie got a laugh out of asking me if that was a factory where they made sass. But there weren't no room for sass with this man. No how.

"Then I ask again." Mr. Dooley started to sound annoyed. "Are we agreed?"

Mr. Vinson stood up, looking all slouched and tired. "Let's vote."

The "yea"s went up in little more than a whisper. No one bothered with the "nay"s. Not even Mr. Vinson. "The 'yea's carry it, Mr. Dooley."

"Very good. I'll be off then." He headed for the door and I wished he'd take me along for fear of what the folks'd have to say to me once he left, but then he said, "Come along, Miss Reid."

Folks looked at me, asking with their eyes, *You aren't siding with that fella, are you?* And just like that everything changed. I didn't want to go nowhere with that man. Wanted to forget I'd ever seen him.

"Miss Reid." His voice took on a hint of threat.

A. LaFaye

Mrs. Wynston gave me a push, whispering, "Go on now."

She knew what that man'd do to me if I said no, but all those other staring eyes had no idea. Those near to seventy faces staring at me, wondering just what I'd done to them.

And it was their eyes that drilled my feet into the ground. "I'm staying, Mr. Dooley."

"What for?" About time he had a bite of the confusion he'd been feeding everyone.

"To talk to folks."

He stepped toward me, his hand on my arm, as his words poured red hot in my ears. "Now is not the time for chatting."

I just couldn't leave with that man, let him come between me and the folks.

"It's unwise for you to stay here." He grabbed my hand and put the squeeze on my fingers. I stepped on his foot, heel down and grinding. He flinched, but kept squeezing. I kept stomping. The two of us pretending it didn't hurt none, but it felt like he might be grinding my fingers down to dust.

Not much more than a few seconds had passed, but the folks had started to stand up, step closer.

"We cannot forever be at odds, Miss Reid. Either you do my bidding or you'll have to leave."

Seeing those folks closing in, knowing they meant only to help me, I started to fear such an act would only make matters worse for them, so I gave in, pulled my foot back and yanked my hand away to march out that door.

My body ached to run, but I wouldn't have that man chase me away, so I just kept marching. He came rushing up behind me, his fingers like pincers on my neck. "It would be in your best interest to stop disobeying me, young lady."

"Mr. Dooley," Mr. Vinson called from behind us.

"Yes, Mr. Vinson." Dooley acted all nice and happy.

"You be wanting me to go over the books with you this evening?"

"Yes, of course. Meet me in the office." He turned back to push me toward the house. Nearly had me tripping over my own feet, he rushed so fast, my neck in his little vise. Once inside, he marched me right up the stairs, opened the door to my room, then stood there waiting.

I stepped inside. Fighting this fella had done wore me down.

"Why not take the evening to consider just how difficult life might be if you keep on your current course?"

Well now, that'd require understanding what he meant by all that, but I didn't say nothing, figuring he'd just get mad at me if I set to asking questions.

He sighed. "Be here when I get back or things will only get worse." As he closed the door, I could've sworn he mumbled, "For both of us," but then he just stomped off.

Thought I'd picked that man out of blind faith, but I'd come to realize my faith had gone blind. I'd done picked the wrong man.

Had me so back to front, I didn't trust my own thoughts, let alone my own prayers. What could I do to get us out of this mess?

The worry of it chewed at me from the inside, sent me to pacing. Near about had me a rut in the floor by the time that fool Dooley come back.

"Good night, Miss Reid." He blew out my lamp, shut the

door, and locked it from his side. I never even knew that door had a lock, let alone seen the key.

I had half a mind to just jump out that window, but with the porch gone I'd fall straight into rubble and probably break my darn neck. Didn't seem too bad an idea just then, but I had folks depending on me.

Staring out the window with nothing but the dark around me, I could see the lights from the Hendersen place. Hattie. Her folks been back from the Adams County Courthouse for a day now. Not a word.

A Wish and a Prayer

No word from Hattie probably meant bad news. I couldn't stand being cooped up in that old room all night not knowing for sure, so I opened the window, used the old support boards for the roof to ease my way over to the oak tree on the corner, climbed onto the branch Daddy had used to sneak into the house as a boy, then worked my way to the ground. Then I hightailed it to Hattie's place to the tune of the tree frogs.

Found everyone to home when I knocked on Hattie's door, but they all looked as thin as if they'd spent the day under a rock pile. Miss Rosie basted a shirt, more piecework she'd been picking up here and there. Mr. Caleb had him a piece of wood he'd been carving a star into. Hattie had socks to darn, probably Hendersen's socks. Could see how she hated them by the way she stabbed in the needle. No one said nary a word, they just kept to their work.

No call asking how things had gone. Could feel it like a ghost in the room, just haunting up the corners, making it seem chilly in there even with the fire just a-blazing. Felt all out of sorts what with them working and me just taking up space, so I headed out to go around back and work in their garden. Wouldn't want me with a needle in my hand 'cause I'd use it 'bout as well as if it were one of Mr. Caleb's chisels and you don't want to see me with no chisel. Give me a hoe and I do just fine.

"You fixing on gardening in the dark?" Hattie asked as she came around the side of their cabin.

"Rosie does it." Known her to do it all night long when she got back from her searching trips—the worry of it all kept her up.

"Adams County weren't no different. Made 'em wait all day, then told 'em they best get out of town before curfew or they'd be arrested."

Made me radish-spitting mad to think on them white folks siding with Hendersen and his evil little contract. Had me right suspicious of them contracts Dooley been going on about. And that talk of arresting and curfew hit me right in the heart. I had a feeling of what that'd be like, having spent the afternoon in the china closet and being locked in my room for the night hours before I'd ever go to bed.

Hattie sat on the rock by the gate her daddy built. He done put a star on that too. For him, stars meant freedom, like following the Drinking Gourd north, only his gourd had been his furniture, him working to have enough to buy his family north. Now with this contract nonsense, I started to wonder if he didn't feel like they'd clouded over the sky, hiding every star from view. How's a body know which way to go if they can't see the stars?

"Daddy says there are more bureau supervisors to see and he'll visit every darn one of them straight to Washington City if that's what it takes." Hattie hugged her knees to her chest. "Mama just keeps on sewing like she'll do just that, right there in that chair, till she dies. Stella, if we don't get out of this place, Mama's heart just going to bust up so bad she'll die from the hurt of it. I can see it in her face."

Thought about telling her about the dream about her brothers, those boys Miss Rosie had lost. Miss Rosie'd be fly-to-the-moon happy to see her boys again. But I couldn't risk having her fall to the earth again if none of them came. Besides, I didn't want to give Hattie another maybe-might-could. So I just hummed me a little tune that Daddy used to sing to quiet me down nights and said me a little prayer on that star in the gate, wishing the Good Lord would show me a way out of the mess I'd done made of Oak Grove, and guide those boys home to Miss Rosie, and steer Mr. Caleb to the right bureau where he could get him a man to declare that contract wrongful. Wood or not, that star looked good enough for wishing. And the only difference between a wish and prayer is the "amen."

A Play for Oak Grove

I prayed to see Miss Rosie's boy walking home in another dream, but I slept straight through until that evil rooster Richardson done pulled me out of bed again—this time, shouting after Mr. Dooley. From a window, I could see him standing just below the veranda, yelling at the house like he expected it to answer. "Show yourself, Conrad Dooley. We have business to discuss."

Dooley come out onto the veranda in one a' them shiny robes that look like he done stole a curtain.

Yanking on his belt, Dooley called down, "And what sort of business did you have in mind, Mr. Richardson? It is Richardson, isn't it?"

Richardson looked like Dooley done spit on him, his face all twisted up with anger. "I'm calling you out to discuss such matters face-to-face." Or avoid going into the house which he still feared on account of the fever.

"Well, I'll admit, I'm not accustomed to your fine Southern traditions, Mr. Richardson, but where I come from it's customary to state your business before you discuss it." He had one a' them

Southern traditions down pat—act friendly, but talk poison.

"My business is your deed, Mr. Dooley. You can't take claim of this place without registering the deed."

"That's a very good point, Mr. Richardson. Now if you'll be so kind as to wait in the parlor, I'll make myself presentable, then you and I can march right down to the land office and I'll take care of that very matter." Still laying on the sugar, Dooley turned to go inside.

Richardson yelled, "I wouldn't be so eager, Mr. Dooley."

"Oh?"

I wished right then that I could just slide out one of the bricks in the wall next to me and chuck it at that no good Richardson. But I had to stand there and listen to all of his hot air and threats. Did that man have his soul removed so he could keep such awful things inside him?

"I'm afraid you'll find it rather difficult. You see, there's a law in this county stating that only registered voters can purchase over one hundred acres of land. Are you a registered voter, Mr. Dooley?"

Like one of them actor types switching costumes in front of a crowd, Mr. Dooley done changed into another person right there on that veranda, going all straight-backed and deep-voiced. "Why, yes, I am, Mr. Richardson. In Massachusetts, New York, Pennsylvania, and Mississippi as of a week ago. Would you like to see my papers?" Mr. Dooley reached for an inside pocket I'm sure he didn't have. That old grandfather law that kept colored folks around here from voting didn't apply to no white folks, so a white man who walked into the state from any old where could register, but a colored man whose family had worked the cotton in Mississippi for a century couldn't so much as try without taking his life in his hands. Where's the justice in that?

Mr. Richardson just stammered like a bee done stung his tongue.

"You see, Mr. Richardson, being a lawyer tends to make one quite accomplished at turning legal matters in their favor. In fact, I believe I can even vote in state matters. Can you?"

Richardson knew darn well he couldn't. Pledging an oath to the Confederacy got him stripped of his voting rights, but he ignored that very idea, saying, "I'd suspect that'd be skilled lawyers who make a living at it, not carpetbagging ones who come waltzing into a fine respectable town to try and snatch up land they've got no right to own."

"Funny you should mention rights, Mr. Richardson, because when legal ownership is under debate, possession wins out until such matters can be settled in court."

All this talk had my heart jumping about like I done swallowed a bird into there. Could Richardson still take Oak Grove? That'd be like going from the bottom of a fire straight to hell.

His hands in fists, his arms going up, Richardson looked ready to sprout wings himself and just fly on up to that veranda and choke that Dooley dead. "You may be sleeping in that house, but you will never own it or the land around it. My family broke the first ground on this property, so it's mine by rights and I aim to claim it, no matter who tries to stand in my way."

The kind of anger that poured off that man could kill. In fact, I had a soul-deep feeling it already had. Something told me Richardson had been the one to kill my daddy. And for that, I wanted him to live with the pain he done caused for the rest of his life. Then let the Lord have him. Ain't no fairer judge than the Lord.

"Let me offer you a little free legal advice, Mr. Richardson. Don't make threats. They'll only harm you in court." If he wasn't so soul-cold awful, I'd almost admire Mr. Dooley for the way he chewed up that old Richardson.

Richardson raised his hand to yell, but spun round and stomped off instead, running at the mouth about stinking Yankees and all that.

Dooley disappeared twice as fast.

I had to know what that man planned to do about this deed business, so I ran into the hall to find out.

Found Dooley at Granddaddy's table eating a breakfast big enough for an ox. "Good morning, Miss Reid. A lady generally dresses for each meal, but considering your clothing predicament, I'll allow you to join me."

Pre-*what?* This man should've come with one of them dictionaries my mama loved so much. I made a note to look up all them fancy words he'd been using.

"You going to sort out the deed?"

Man ate with his knife and his fork like he expected the food to get uppity or something. Setting them down all careful, he said, "I don't much care for repeating myself, Miss Reid, but I'll remind you again that Oak Grove is mine now and I'll thank you to mind your own business."

I wished I could thank him for getting out of my family's house and off their land, but I had to sit there and watch that buzzard eat.

Mr. Dooley asked, "So, what schools have you attended?"

"None."

"Pardon?"

"Never been."

"Who was your tutor?"

I figured tutor to be a teaching word, so I said, "My mama."

"Good heavens. You've had no formal schooling?" He shook his head. "No wonder your cousin wishes to see me on the matter."

Sounded like he thought I'd never so much as stepped foot in a church in my life. Never met anybody who made schooling sound so holy.

"Can you read and write?"

"Yes." *And I can stand on my head, too. Want to see it, you coot?*

"What do you know of history? Philosophy? Music?"

I knew near about everything that ever happened on Oak Grove. Besides, as I told him, "Don't need none of that for planting and harvesting."

"You mean to tell me you work this plantation?"

I nodded.

"Good heavens." He scowled at me.

Boy, I'd sure painted myself the sinner in his eyes and all before he'd finished his breakfast. But right about then, he looked like he might be figuring something, probably where he could ship me off to.

But he got up, went to the dresser, then came back with a book I knew well. Daddy's log book. My hands just itched to have that back.

He dropped that book in front of me and opened it to the first page I'd written on. Pointing to my initials, he said, "Is that you?"

"Yes, sir." Only one letter marked me from Daddy, the *E* for my middle name, Evelyne, instead of his *B* for Benton.

He flipped through pages real quicklike. "All of this is you?"

I wrote down everything I heard, everything I'd learned from watching Daddy and the others, plus a few things I knew on my own.

He opened that book to a planting map I'd drawn, then started to pace. "You discuss crop rotation, pest control, projected harvests, even planting patterns to maximize yield. There are plans and maps for how to fight fires in here." He looked nervous, even scared—the idea a girl like me could do all that had him on the run, inside and out.

He squatted down quite close to me. "These are your ideas?"

"Most are said in meeting."

He stood up with a snorting kind of laugh. "Some of the greatest minds in the world have struggled to build their own utopias and a little backwoods country girl from Mississippi has lived in one all of her life. Writing down her observations in a style that'd practically put Thoreau himself to shame. After all, he couldn't draw worth spit." He laughed, a punch-in-the-gut kind of laugh that made me jump.

I didn't know a "utopia" from a stick in the mud, but I liked that look in his eyes, like he could see me regular now. Not as a girl who should be in a dress, but as Stella Reid. I didn't have the right to step into my daddy's shoes, but I'd done what I could to hold the place together.

"You have talents, my dear girl. Talents." He smiled like he just might take to the idea of having me do the work I'd always been doing.

I had an itching to be out in the fields, doing my share of the work, so the folk'd know I wasn't siding with that Dooley fella one bit. And come nightfall, I could go to meeting feeling like I belonged. Before bed, I'd write in the log. That is, if I could ever get it back.

He stood at the window, clutching that book like he thought it held something special, not just a recording of all we done over the last few years. "This meeting system of yours has actually run this place?"

Seemed right obvious to me, especially since every darn person who met him since he'd stepped onto the property told him the same said thing.

He pointed to the book. "It says here your father died before the last harvest. You detailed everything they did to bring in the cotton, pick the orchard, even cure meat for winter. Why you? Why not your mother or that foreman fellow, Vinson?"

Mama never tended to anything on the plantation itself, except her garden and them bees. Beyond that, she kept to the house. "Mama never took to being a planter. Mr. Vinson keeps his own books."

"Not like this one. This is an almanac."

Whatever that was.

"And the folks here decided what to do based on those meetings?" He kept asking me that. Why didn't the idea of meetings fit inside that head of his?

"That's right."

He nodded, looking as happy as a boy at the candy counter. "Well then, there's no need to stop sound business practices." Putting the book in front of me, he said, "Keep writing."

"And we'll still have meetings?"

"Of course." He walked to the door. "Now, if you'll excuse me. I must dress and check in with Mr. Vinson. After that, you and I have to go into town and get some proper clothing for you."

Proper to him meant torture to me, but at least I'd be there when he made a go of filing that deed. With his iron ways, he just might get it done.

That Mr. Dooley sure turned out to be a fine puzzlement. Proper this. Proper that. Then all his talk of them utopia's like we done something true special at Oak Grove. That had him all happy just a-moving and flowing like them rules was just a hard crust keeping the real of him locked inside. Made me wonder if them rules of his just might crack given enough pressure. But I'd sure have to be careful in the finding out if I wanted to stay out of the china closet.

So I had to get to stepping. Taking up the log book felt like holding on to a piece of my daddy. I could near about smell him in the leather. As I passed Mr. Dooley at the door, he said, "Come next week, you'll start your schooling, young lady. I won't have an idiot as my ward."

Anytime I started to feel the least bit good, he done poured the bad right back down my throat. Calling me an idiot. Now, I knew that word. Meant I weren't no smarter than a rock. Well, if he felt that way, why'd he even want me to keep the log? Had me so mad, I near about threw it back at him, but when I turned around, he said, "I meant that in the Greek sense of the word, my dear. Among the Greeks, an idiot was a person who knew only his own culture."

Well then, he'd called it right because I had no idea what he meant by "culture," let alone them fellas called "Greeks," so maybe I was an idiot. But I still felt a tiny flame of happiness spark up inside me. Saw the smallest sliver of a chance that Mr. Dooley might come to our way of seeing things. And I planned to do all I could to make that chance grow like a flower planted deep in manure. Yes, sir. Just grow and grow and grow till we had so many flowers, we don't know what to do with 'em. Well, a girl can dream, can't she?

A Series of Startlements

I made sure I beat Mr. Dooley to Mr. Vinson, so he and I had a chance to talk. Poor man looked fit to be hog-tied and thrown in the river. "Things be bad, Miss Stella. Real bad. Folks talking of tearing down the cabins and moving on."

Tearing them down? But why? They'd worked side by side with Daddy to build those places, set their names in stone over their doors. Why would they want to take them down?

"Folks been calling them places their own. Now that Dooley fella says they be his."

And if they tore them down, they belonged to nobody.

"Least with sharecropping we'd be living in our own house."

"We?" The idea of Mr. Vinson leaving had me unsteady like he'd knocked a support beam out from under me.

"Now, don't you fret." He patted my shoulder, but didn't look so sure, pacing his office like he did. "Folks set to panic like this when your daddy died. I calmed them then. I'll calm them now."

"Tell them Dooley took to meetings. Real meetings. Not like he done last night."

"You sure?"

I patted the log. "Thinks they're right fine now."

He took that log and kissed it. "Art, I told you. Art."

I smiled. He laughed.

"Good morning, Mr. Vinson." Dooley knocked on the open door, then stepped in. "Miss Reid."

He gave me a *what-are-you-doing-here* kind of look, but I just kept right on praying that he'd stick to his word.

"Well, Mr. Vinson, I've had time to review that log that Miss Reid here has kept." He eyed me real suspicious-like. "And . . . well, I must say, I . . ."

If he had to say it so bad, why didn't he just say it?

"I must say you've all done an exceedingly good job with the place. I'm willing to give this meeting system of yours a real try. Keep the reporting and voting system you've been using."

He started to get a little pink in the cheeks and it wasn't even hot yet. That stiff-as-a-metal-rod man had gotten embarrassed. He felt ashamed to admit we'd been doing things right all along. Thought of pushing things a little and asking after the houses, but then Mr. Vinson started shaking that man's hand like he already done give us a piece of heaven, so I decided to wait for another time. Another crack in that fella's steel mask.

"That's fine, real fine, sir." Mr. Vinson just kept shaking that hand. "I'll be telling folks today. They'll be ready for voting come sundown."

"Very well, then." Now that Dooley looked white. Had he gone scared? If he had, he wasn't going to show it. He turned, took my elbow and led me out the door quicklike. "Come, Miss Reid. We must get to town."

And *whoosh*, off we went. He had Mr. Zachariah hitch up a

horse to a surrey, a traveling contraption I'd never seen before, and we set to a-bouncing off down the road. Those old two-seaters sure did ride smooth.

We made our first stop at the Farlington's, that squeaky-floored place where they sold dresses from places like Paris and London and New York, all for prices fit for a whole bale a' cotton, all four hundred pounds of it. Nobody with good sense should be spending that kind of money on no little petticoat of a dress full of frilly froufrou nonsense.

"Now, Miss Reid, we'll get you started, then I'll head over to the land office and pick you up when I'm through. You should get three dresses. Two for everyday and one for special occasions. I'm afraid that's all we can afford at this time."

It'd be much cheaper to get me none.

Mrs. Farlington, the owner and seamstress, didn't seem to take the idea of us buying a dress neither. She came out and stood at the counter with her arms folded over her chest like a cotton buyer, all sour face and *you-ain't-going-to-get-no-deals-from-me*.

"Good day." Dooley put on the big smile.

"'Morning." She kind of breathed out the word.

"We're here for a few dresses for Miss Reid."

"I see. Well, I'm afraid you'll have to go elsewhere."

"I beg your pardon?"

"With times as they are, Mr. Dooley, we've had to limit our sales to *loyal* customers."

I figured she meant those loyal to the Confederacy.

"My loyalties may be blue, madam, but I assure you, my money is pure gold."

"Don't care if it's diamonds. We aren't selling to no Yankees."

"Come, Miss Reid." He turned me right around and marched out the door. Once he hit the boardwalk, he let out a string of words no man should say before God.

Straightening his vest, he said, "I do apologize, Miss Reid, but prejudice burns me to the bone."

If that little scene upset him, he had a heap of hurt coming his way. That sort of thing seemed like a kiss on the cheek compared to what people did to the colored folks in these parts—beating them for "looking" at a white girl, declaring their children orphans and working them to the bone, or burning their business to the ground for opening their doors to the public. That little thing in the store weren't no thing atall in my way of thinking.

"Miss Rosie can sew a dress they'd bury the queen in."

"What queen?"

Man didn't know a figure of speech when he heard it? "Any, I guess. I just meant she sews good."

"She sews 'well,' my dear. She sews 'well.'"

It's all well and good to me.

"On to the land office, then."

And off we went. Things seemed to go pretty *well* until the clerk took the man behind us in line, then Mr. Dooley kind of elbowed the fella out of the way and said to the clerk, "Pardon me, sir, but this gentleman was behind me in line."

"This gentleman"—the clerk took up the fella's papers—"has been farming land in this town since you were still trying to learn to spell your own name."

"How is that a fair measure for service?"

"It's a lot fairer than a fella coming in to buy land he got no right to."

And that set the tone for things. Planters and farmers alike came in with this claim or that, going ahead of Mr. Dooley again and again.

Didn't take but five of them folks for Mr. Dooley to yell, "Do you ever plan to take my claim, sir?"

"Not atall," said the clerk. The fellas in line laughed.

"Then I'll just have to take my business to the county seat."

Mr. Dooley grabbed my arm and set to march out all dignified, but the clerk shouted, "You do that, sir. Give my best to Clemet Eastman, the county clerk!"

I felt Mr. Dooley's arm slump.

"I've never seen such rude behavior in my life," he said as we stepped outside.

I had. And Mr. Caleb and Miss Rosie sure knew it better than anyone.

"Mr. Caleb and Miss Rosie done waited all day in bureau after bureau to get a contract old Hendersen put on Hattie ruled illegal. They haven't had one plug of luck."

"Pardon me?"

Now, I may not like to talk much, but I hated to repeat myself.

"Nobody willing to say the contract claiming Hattie's an orphan is wrong."

"Why not?"

Man, this fella sure had put the idiot mask on for the day. "They're colored."

"Oh, of course." He shook his head. "My father always said Southerners had their own sense of the law. I'm beginning to see just what he meant."

That father of his seemed a right smart fella. I almost wished he was the one to come south and not his son. Especially after the younger Dooley had me explain Mr. Caleb and Miss Rosie's whole situation on the way to Cousin Mertle's.

But I have to lay claim to the fact I had a bit of the devil in me that day 'cause I felt kind a' eager to see just how old Dooley fared with Miss Mertle and that Miss Shaw. Thought that woman would turn into a ghost straightaway she went so pale when she seen Mr. Dooley at the door. "Good evening," she piped, sounding like she done swallowed a whistle or something. "I mean, good morning."

"Good day, madam. Is the woman of the house at home?"

Where would she be? Woman's as old as a tree.

"Yes, sir. Whom shall I say is calling?"

Why, blast it all, if those two wouldn't get on like two turtles on a log in the sun. All "madams" and "sirs" and such. That'll teach me to let the devil in.

"Conrad Dooley of Oak Grove most recently, but I come here by way of the law firm of Fitz, Heller, and Wells of Philadelphia."

"A lawyer? How fine."

How was I supposed to live through those two going all sweet and fluttery?

"Thank you, madam."

I would've liked to thank him for letting me stay outside, but no, we got shuffled in to see Cousin Mertle, who acted like I done brought home one of them college teachers she went on about with Daddy when she talked on her husband being a doctor and all.

Those two got to chatting about who wrote this book and

made that kind of music on what kind of instrument. Never been so bored in all my days. Think I'd rather count ants coming out of a hill.

"Why, Stella, you have done your family right proud to have secured yourself such a benefactor." She patted Mr. Dooley's hand like they was old friends. And here I thought she didn't take to Yankees atall. But no, she seemed to like Mr. Dooley right fine. Even used his calling name. "Now, Conrad, I know she is a rough-hewn ward, but I swear on her mother's grave, she is a good-hearted girl who will make a fine woman."

Didn't like nobody swearing on Mama's grave and I prayed I'd never be considered fine in all my days. Then I noticed Miss Shaw sitting on the piano bench looking all dazed and blurry-eyed. *Oh my, just bury me now.*

"She does have potential."

Po-what? Add another word to that list I got growing in my head.

"She certainly does."

"And our first step is to get her some proper clothing."

Miss Mertle actually clapped her hands like a young girl at a barn dance. "Oh, fine. I should send Katherine upstairs; I'm sure I have plenty of clothing that would suit her."

Dooley smiled, but his eyes had the look of starlement. "Oh, I do believe you've given her quite enough already with your investment in Oak Grove. And I plan to see she gets every penny of it in the way of a good education."

Miss Mertle sighed real happylike. "I'm certain you will, Conrad. And I expect to see you back here for supper come Sunday."

"Wouldn't have it any other way."

He shuffled me out the door and shoot me dead for I'm lying, if he didn't say, "I hope that Miss Shaw is a better cook than a conversationalist. I've met more lively chairs."

Didn't know a conver-*what's it* from a congregation, but I knew he'd done called Miss Shaw as boring as wood. And that came out sounding about right to me.

Then we went out to the Hendersen place so he could put in an order for a few dresses for me. We waited outside Hattie's cabin after he knocked and when Miss Rosie come out, Mr. Dooley offered his hand and even tipped his head, saying, "It's good to meet you, Miss Rose. I'm Mr. Dooley."

"Miss Rose" sounded so nice and he tipped his head like he'd met a lady on the boardwalk. Made my heart warm to have him treat her so nice.

She just got all blushy and shy, bowing her head.

"I need three dresses for Miss Reid here."

"Dresses?" She looked confused.

"Yes, dresses."

Miss Rosie looked at me, then at him. She'd been sewing my britches since I took to the fields.

"Do you need to take her measurements?"

"No, sir. I know them." But she didn't believe the order, not by the look on her face.

"Maybe they could be riding dresses?" I asked. "I mean the ones for day-to-day. Give me a chance to get used to dresses."

He shook his head, then sighed. "For now."

Made me feel so darn good I jumped over and kissed his cheek before I knew what I'd done. He turned five shades of red and I probably tried out a few of my own. Miss Rosie just laughed, then covered her mouth, saying, "Sorry."

He cleared his throat and stiffened, the iron pouring back into him. "Well, do send me a bill when you have the dresses done."

"Yes, sir."

"And Miss Rose, I've heard of your legal troubles. I'll see what I can do."

"You will?" The happy in Miss Rosie's eyes looked to be enough to make her float.

"He's a lawyer." And he better be a darn good one or I'd tan his hide for leading Miss Rosie on.

"He is?"

He patted her hand like he wanted to push that idea back. "Now, I'm not well-versed with Mississippi law, but I will see what I can do."

"We'd be mighty grateful. Mighty grateful." She squeezed his hand.

That made him smile. "I'd be glad to help."

He walked back to the surrey all puffed up and happy. Why, Mr. Dooley actually liked helping folks. Weren't that a startlement fit to make a bird forget how to fly. That man had him more secrets than a family of five daughters. I set to wondering just what else he had hidden up his sleeve.

Smoke

I dreamt of numbers and dials and the slow metal clicking of the safe handle being turned—my mind searching for the right combination for that blasted safe. For a change, Mrs. Wynston woke me up real excited-like: "Miss Stella, Miss Stella, there a man here asking after Miss Rosie."

"Miss Rosie?" For a bit I wondered why anyone would come to Oak Grove looking for Miss Rosie, then I remembered my letters and the walking dream. I ran down those stairs so fast, I near about took the skin off the bottoms of my feet.

Found a fella standing at my front door holding his hat, looking all lost and nervous.

"How do." I stayed by the front door, not wanting him to feel any more nervous than he already did.

"You the lady that write about a Rosie mama looking for her boys?"

I nodded.

"She had her three sons?"

A nod. I played things nice and easy, but inside I be running and jumping for joy.

"You sure none of them sons called Jonah?"

I'd heard her repeat them names a thousand times, Isaac, Jacob, Abraham. No way I'd remember them wrong.

"See, I be a Jonah and my mama done been sold off when I weren't nothing but a baby. Folks say her name be Rosie. I don't remember her, but to know I miss her." He kept staring at his hands as they turned that hat around.

He could've been spinning my heart for how bad it felt, knowing he weren't one of Miss Rosie's boys and that she weren't his mama. Even if I had the Jacob wrong, he would've been the middle child, a field worker, when she left. Not a baby.

"I'm real sorry, Mr. Jonah, but I don't think my Miss Rosie's your mama. She had her a Jacob. Not a Jonah."

"You sure?" He looked about ready to cry.

I nodded.

He turned, looking all dragged out and small.

"Mr. Jonah?"

"Yessum?"

"You need you any work?" I nodded to the fields. With all the folks that'd been leaving, we needed the hands in the fields, especially come harvest and that weren't but a few months away. "We got plenty of work around here. Fella that owns the place even giving salary."

"Cash money?"

"That's right."

He started spinning that hat right fast. "I should be finding my mama."

"We can help you do that from right here."

"Really?" He looked like he might do a backflip on the very spot where he stood.

"Yes, sir."

"Why thank ya, thank ya kindly."

"Go on down to the foreman's cabin. He's got him a blue gate." I pointed that-a-way. "Name of Mr. Vinson. He'll get you situated."

"Thank ya!" He bowed and ran off.

"Be sure to tell him about your mama!"

"Yessum. I will!"

He weren't Miss Rosie's boy, but I did feel pretty good signing him on, knowing we done found a few lost mamas in our day. Why, Mr. Zachariah had lost his Maggie and their oldest children before he came to Oak Grove, but we tracked her down and bought her home.

"What did you just do?" Mr. Dooley's voice done spun me around like he had me on a string. He leaned over the veranda railing, looking all mean and angry like one of them stone fellas on that fancy library Daddy took me to in New Orleans.

"Hired a man."

"What makes you think you have such a right?"

"Fact I know we don't have enough hands to bring in the cotton come harvest."

"And do you know if I have the money to pay that man?"

"Pay or no pay, you'll be needing him."

"That's for me to decide, Miss Reid."

Held my breath for a second, trying to keep all the anger from spilling out of my mouth, then I asked, "You won't send him off, will you?"

"I should to teach you a lesson, but I'm not making that man pay for your mistakes."

Phew.

"But I'll be sure that you do."

My payment for that mistake was scrubbing every floor in that house on my hands and knees. Whoever said housework didn't amount to fieldwork didn't spend no days on their knees. I had muscles aching I never knew to name.

Come sundown, I had to have me a little rest. Just shut my eyes and rested my bones a bit.

Mr. Dooley shook my shoulder, saying, "Miss Reid."

I woke up with a muscle-hurting rattle. Place looked as dark as a root cellar 'cept for his lamp. "I miss the meeting?"

"Just over. And a young lady such as yourself should do well to get some rest before the work that lays ahead tomorrow."

I followed Mr. Dooley toward our bedrooms. Felt like asking him how things went, but I'd learned not to be asking too many questions. Funny how a man like Dooley made me want to talk, but didn't allow it. Now that was a switch.

"Miss Reid."

I turned to face him as we stood across the hall from each other, hoping he didn't have any more ugly things to say.

"Have you seen . . . oh, heavens, what is that man's name? He always wears that beaten-down old hat."

"Mr. Quincy, he's the head of the north field crew."

"Right." Mr. Dooley snapped his fingers in recognition. "Well, he wasn't at the meeting tonight. Folks were asking after him. You wouldn't have seen him, have you?"

Never crossed Mr. Quincy's path on most days, but he'd been threatening to leave since Daddy had died, so I didn't find his absence that big a startlement. "No, sir."

"All right." Mr. Dooley nodded, then headed into his room. "Good night."

Dressing for bed, I heard Mr. Dooley talking. Thought maybe he had him a guest in there, but no one answered him and he talked in a steady kind of way, like he might be preaching.

I leaned into the wall to have a listen.

"In this case, we have to consider not just the letter of the law, but the intent. When Mr. Lincoln established the rights of the Negroes, he sought to have them regarded as our equals."

He'd started speechifying about rights. Did he mean to use it to help Mr. Caleb and Miss Rosie? One of her boys walking home and now a real chance at getting Hattie back—why, Miss Rosie would be thinking she'd already been called home to Jesus. Near about wanted to run in there and thank Mr. Dooley for his part in it all, but I didn't get a chance.

The shout went up. Folks yelling, "Fire! Fire!"

Mr. Dooley and I nearly collided as we both ran for the main stairs. "Stay here, Miss Reid. For your safety."

"I done put me a fire out already, how about you?" I asked, beating him to the back door. He may be tall, but he sure didn't run that good. I'd made it halfway down to the quarters before he caught up.

But no kind of speed could stop what I seen. The flames just a-eating away at them brick cabins from the inside, folks standing in the road watching their homes go up into the sky. Someone'd waited for Mr. Dooley to head to the house, knowing the folk'd still be in the meeting hall talking about the day. No one about to see them start the fires. Why, those sheet-wearing, soulless fiends. They deserved to be roasted over such a fire as the ones they'd set that night.

Even with the cabins too far gone, we had a much bigger problem. The cotton. Soon as the shock wore off, folks ran for water, ladies pumping at the troughs and wells like it'd keep them breathing, others wetting blankets to stomp down the sparks and flames that flew away from the cabins. Mr. Vinson started him a shovel team for the north side, I ran for the south side and met up with Mr. Zachariah leading a mess of fellas ready to fight fire.

Had me a shovel in hand when I seen Mr. Dooley spinning this way and that, asking, "What do I do?"

"Start digging!" I yelled as Mr. Harris threw him my shovel.

He dug in right behind me, asking, "What are we doing?"

"Digging a trench to fill with water. If that fire don't jump it, the flames'll go out before they reach the fields."

"I see."

That man may know his Greeks from his idiots, but he sure didn't know how to fight a fire. From lightning to a sleepy pipe-smoker, we'd had more than our share a' fires on Oak Grove, but never two in a month. That Richardson meant what he said about being sure no one be standing in his way. Probably figured he could burn them cabins and blame it on the folks. Didn't need them if'n he planned on sharecropping.

I didn't have no time to be dwelling on that evil toad. Had me a ditch to dig. My arms had been scrubbing all day and near about gave out on me, but I kept on praying, kept on pushing, and followed right behind Mr. Harris who dug in front of me. Had no time to keep an eye on Mr. Dooley, just kept digging.

First roof to cave pulled me up short. What a sight to see a body's home go to the ground like that. Why, that'd been Pastor Rallsom's cabin. His missus done died in that cabin—the first place they had to call their own in all the years they'd been married.

Had no time to mourn no building, though. That fire done started to grab at the tufts of grass in the road, jump from the roofs for the cotton. Ditch wouldn't do us no good if the sparks jumped it, but we kept digging, folks doing the jumping to head into the fields with buckets to wet the cotton.

"Got sparks!" shouted a spotter from the meeting house roof. "Northeast corner field two!"

Folks went a-running, wet blankets in tow to slap those flames down.

Took us near to dawn, but we fought that fire down to ash. 'Course the lot of us looked just about as bad by then. Me, I couldn't stop coughing.

'Fore I knew it, Mr. Dooley done called folks in to wrap me up in blankets and cart me off to bed. Mrs. Wynston sat up with me as I fought to get that smoke outta my lungs. Darn if that stuff didn't stick into you like prickers.

Ain't no worse feeling than coughing for air and getting none. Had me on my knees like a dog, panting between coughs, begging for air.

Mrs. Wynston went running for a doctor.

My head got all swimmy, but I fought to keep my senses, fearing I'd stop breathing if I passed out.

Felt Mrs. Wynston take me in her arms and rock me, her saying, "Don't you take Stella, Lord. Don't you take her. She got living to do yet, Lord. Good living."

Even heard Mr. Dooley yelling at somebody. Had all those people fighting on my behalf. Felt like I could let go a little. Give in to that cloud filling my head. So I did.

Heaven and Hell

All that smoke I took in kept a hold on me for near to a week. Had me coughing and sleeping and not much else. Mr. Dooley had me carried out to the veranda for fresh air each morning, with Hattie leading the way talking about the Queen of Sheba on account of them carrying me in the air like that. But I slept through most everything. All that coughing done takes a lot out of a body. Of course I didn't sleep but no time atall before I started coughing again.

And when I wasn't making all kinds of racket I could hear Mr. Dooley going on about something. Always something, but I never could keep my mind free of sleep long enough to hear what had him going on.

Miss Shaw done come around to see to me on Cousin Mertle's request and all of Mr. Dooley's carrying on sent her right out of her chair to whisper at him. Maybe she meant to shush him for keeping me up, but from all the giggling Hattie done when Miss Shaw did that, I figure she be putting a little courting into her nursing. And the thought of that nonsense sure enough put me back to sleep.

A. LaFaye

By the time my lungs finally got clear of all that smoke, I felt like I'd been fighting that fire for days, every muscle I had all charred up and sore. But I didn't look near as bad as Mr. Quincy when Mr. Harris, our carpenter, and Mr. Zachariah brought him home.

"Found him in the creek," said Mr. Zachariah.

I heard it more than seen it, 'cause I couldn't look at Mr. Quincy's poor broken-up body, all cuts, bruises, and bleeding. Miss Isabella hovered over him, trying to ease his aches as he moaned. All that pain and he just kept whispering, "I'm sorry, I'm sorry." Probably begging the people who hurt him to stop.

Poor man couldn't open his left eye, it'd swollen up so bad. Had him broken ribs and maybe even a bleed on the inside according to Mrs. Wynston, who did the doctoring 'cause Dr. Aaronson, the only doctor in Helensburg, done refused to even come out to Oak Grove. That must've been what had Mr. Dooley yelling while I lay sick—no doctor would come see me. No big trouble there. Mrs. Wynston best doc I knew.

"Ridiculous," Mr. Dooley yelled, pacing outside the office where we had Mr. Quincy resting. "A man of healing should have a code of ethics. How can he allow someone to just die?"

Mr. Vinson stood there with his arms crossed and his back bowed. "Maybe that's his idea of ethics, letting *particular* people die."

Richardson done set the town against us, and Mr. Quincy had to pay for it. The fires, the beating of Mr. Quincy, and the noose Richardson tightened around Oak Grove each day—all of it had me working that safe so hard you'd think I was trying to crack it with the sheer force of how fast I turned that dial again and

198

again. Finally, I stomped out of the office mad enough to blow that thing up with my thoughts.

What I should've done was pool in with the folks of Oak Grove. Then we all could've bought land upriver where they didn't charge so much. We could've had a good spread. Wouldn't nobody be busted up or living in the barn, the stables, the meeting house, and any old where we could find some room until we had some lumber. Lumber folks in Helensburg wouldn't sell to us. We didn't have no sawmill like the Hendersens, so Mr. Garrett Beeman and his boys had to head Natchez way to get us some wood—what little wood we could afford. Mr. Dooley done spent most of the money buying the darn place.

The whole of it dropped me to the stoop in exhaustion.

Mr. Vinson sat down next me. He patted my knee. "Don't you go blaming yourself, Miss Stella. Mr. Quincy brought this on his own self."

I stared at him.

"That right." He nodded toward the rubble of charred bricks where the cabins once stood. "You see him that night?"

I shook my head.

"People saying they done paid him to set that fire. Give him his own land. When he go to collect, this what they done."

The idea had me torn up one side and down the other. Mr. Quincy hurting us? I didn't want to believe it. Didn't want to know he could. But I hated them low-down snakes for playing on a man's desire to have something of his own. Weren't too many plantations left where the folks hadn't taken down the old quarters, so those dirty dogs knew such a fire would have a nasty kind of pull on Mr. Quincy, especially after Mr. Dooley done told all the folks he owned them cabins the folks of Oak Grove had as their own since they'd built them. Then those soulless fiends had to go and lie to Mr. Quincy, telling him they'd give him land, then beating him for wanting it.

Had to walk. Try my hand at outrunning all the ugliness building up around me—the lies, the fires, the beating, the shutout from town. What for? Land. Stinking land that gave out a little more cotton than most. How could that Richardson put out so much hate and still go on living and breathing like he had a right to it?

"Don't you even think on it," Hattie said from a roost on the garden well.

I stopped, knowing she could see how much I wanted to just keep walking, leave Oak Grove behind me, give all them folks to God and pray He could show them the way to their own happiness.

"You think I come here for your friendship." She dropped the package she carried onto the ledge, then jumped down. "No, sir. I come here because ain't no thing that can stop Miss Stella Reid. Not losing her papa. Not yellow fever. Not losing her mama. Not even fire. That girl just keep on fighting. If she can keep on, I can too. That's why I come here." She pulled the package off the ledge. "That and Mama's done with your dresses." She threw the package at me.

"Thanks, Hattie." She gave me a little bit a' pride wrapped up in a laugh. Not every friend can do that for a girl.

"Don't thank me until you see them dresses. They look downright girl-like."

I rolled my eyes.

"They think that skunk going to live?"

How'd she know about Mr. Quincy?

"Girl, he been talking up that deal he made all over the Hendersen place, going from sharecropper to sharecropper. If'n you ask me, he got what he deserve, burning them houses down, and being dumb enough to trust a white man." She shook her head.

Good thing God didn't consult the likes of her about Mr. Quincy. Sure, he done wrong, but no man deserved that kind of pain, except maybe Richardson. No, not even him. I couldn't wish that moaning-through-the-night kind of pain on anyone. Mr. Quincy's wife, Miss Isabella, gave him the aspirin powder Mr. Dooley give her, but it didn't do no good.

So I set to trying to do the only good I could at the time. I started praying and writing letters to find Jonah's Rosie. Said he last knew of her down Macon way, so I wrote one to the bureau in Macon. One to the post office there. Then I wrote to as many bureaus I knew of between Macon and Oak Grove. Well, I should say, I did them letters until Mr. Dooley's hollering pulled me away.

Mr. Dooley started pacing the back of the house, yelling, "This place is run by pure madness. I expect the middle of the African jungle to be a safer place than here. I'd even face a lion rather than this nonsense."

Now, that is a figure of speech. No man with any sense in his head would face a lion by choice.

"If the Masai can do it, so can I." His voice fell to a whisper as he said, "At least then, I'd have a fighting chance to prove myself."

He knew of folks that fought lions? My heavens. Maybe being an idiot weren't such a bad idea after all. I didn't want to hear about how other people got themselves hurt. I had enough trouble seeing it happen to people I knew.

But I remember one thing from another *culture*; see, I'd looked that word up and knew it meant the way of doing and believing among other people, so I figured that old saying my daddy got from a Chinese herb-selling man came from another culture. That man told Daddy they had a saying over China way. It said, "This too shall pass." Whatever's happening only has a short life to live, something else'll come along and live in its spot. So even the worst of times going to pass away.

And the days did pass like cotton grows, strands forming from sunrise to sunset till the bolls crack open and start to dry. Folks just kept pushing forward, trying to outlast that blasted Richardson.

Mr. Quincy healing up inside, but fighting to take his medicine for his sins, working side by side with the folks he done wronged, sleeping outside even in the rain, and giving his salary back to Mr. Dooley for the lumber we needed. Could've built a few cabins at a time, but folks voted on waiting until they had enough for everyone. Then we could build them on the plots they had laid out around their cotton land.

Everyone worked hard to keep going. When they finished the fields already in cotton, they turned to the fallow land to work in manure and get it ready for planting come planting time. Felt soul-good to see the kind of spirit I loved about Oak Grove, doing everything like a family—even their punishment, knowing Quincy'd never learn nothing but guilt if he left Oak Grove, so they worked right along with him, feeding him meals, treating him firm, but regular, showing they hated the actions, but not the man.

I had to agree with Mr. Beeman—Oak Grove was like a slice of heaven and that old devil Richardson sought to destroy it, but he didn't burn us out and we could make do without his doctors or his lumber. What we couldn't do was get the cotton to market without going through Helensburg. Richardson would have that town sewn up like a hidden money belt—he'd never let us get the cotton through to market. I feared the harvest like a hurricane coming in off the gulf, threatening to tear up everything we done worked to keep growing.

With June ending and July beginning, we had only a month to sort things out. Wasn't no shortage on trying. Mr. Caleb and Miss Rosie spent every day they had free and even a few they traded for, sitting in bureaus waiting on the paper that would declare that contract wrongful and set Hattie free. Mr. Dooley, when he weren't working to make beds or it'll-do walls for the folks or getting him the know-how of growing cotton, or teaching me something, he went to that county courthouse to try and file his deed or get someone to listen to his call for a hearing on behalf of Mr. Caleb and Miss Rosie, but he couldn't find him a judge who'd listen to their case or his.

Meanwhile, I kept writing letters after Miss Rosie's boys and Jonah's Rosie, working the fields when Mr. Dooley went away, and studying. Mr. Dooley insisted on studying, but he wouldn't let me go to school with the children down in the meeting house. Said I was too old for the work they'd be doing with that schoolteacher he hired from down New Orleans way. No, I had to be studying history, philosophy, mathematics (that's what he called figuring), and music with Mr. Dooley himself. And let me tell you, some of them books was more boring than watching bread go moldy, but I liked that piano playing. Could even drum me out a tune or two. Turned out Mr. Beeman's Garrett know'd a world a' songs on the piano and he taught me a few.

And I'd be lying if I didn't admit to liking quite a bit of that book learning—finding out about that Queen of Sheba Hattie went on about and folks over in Asia and Europe—they even have a place called Tasmania where they got little critters they call devils, but they ain't got no horns.

On the subject of telling the truth, I'd have to say Mr. Dooley had him a good way of teaching, being all patient and quiet, asking questions instead of yelling. When I watched his face, all calm and eager for me to learn, I got to feeling a funny kind of warm, like it might just be right to have him sitting there beside me, guiding me along.

That's when thoughts of Mama made me feel bad, like I done something to her by getting to feel regular with Mr. Dooley. Made me want to slam the book on his fingers, but Mama would've wanted me learning, so I kept right on reading, and reading, and reading. Got so deep into my studies, I burned down more than one wick.

One night, Mr. Dooley came in to turn down my lamp and send me to bed.

"But I got more studying to do."

"That's, 'I *have* more studying to do,'" Mr. Dooley said, holding up my covers. "And there's plenty of time for that tomorrow, because you can't change the world in a day, my dear. You have to do it one thing at a time."

Well, one day or a thousand, I did enjoy learning all that stuff. Kind of filled my mind up, gave less room to my worries.

But when Mr. Vinson fired up the gin to keep it limber and said we'd probably need new belts, my worries got so big they could push any new fact outta their way. Most years we could order the parts in town, but now we'd have to go buy them elsewhere. And I didn't trust the roads in these parts. One of our loads of lumber had ended up on its side, the boards strewn and cracked, the driver, Mr. Harris, knocked over the head. Richardson done declared war on us and we had no way to stop him.

The hopelessness of it all had folks working real slow, not talking much, and keeping the meetings short. Mr. Dooley even took to disappearing nights. Walking in the dark. I prayed none of Richardson's folks would hear tell of that and jump him.

I'd taken to pacing the veranda so I could hear if he called out, when somebody else yelled out from below. Had me on my feet in a flash and looking down to see if it weren't a messenger sent to tell me they'd found Mr. Dooley in the creek or on the road or some awful thing.

"Sorry if I startled you," said the man down below.

In the dark, couldn't see much of him, so I told him to wait there and ran down. Opening the door, I saw a man around the age of Mrs. Wynston's daughter, Mary Ellen, standing there straightening out his coat and pulling at loose threads. The whole thing looked ready to come apart with a good tug, but I wasn't one to talk, I had to wear a dress like some sissified girl. Least Miss Rosie made me riding skirts, so they had a split down the middle of the skirt and moved a bit like britches.

And it turned out to be Miss Rosie this young man wanted.

"I'm Abe. Come from Biloxi. A letter say you know a Rosie who had a man named Earl and three boys."

Had me breathing so hard, you'd a thought I'd fought another fire. "Yes, sir."

"Them boys, you say be Isaac, Jacob, and Abraham. That's me. Had me two older brothers by them names. Said they called our poppy Earl."

"They did?" My heart set to dancing. Dear Lord, let him be Miss Rosie's hickory baby.

"Never do 'member my mama. Say she had to give me to a nursing mammy 'fore they took her away."

He looked about ready to cry.

"Said her name be Rosie." He kicked the step. "Ya know my mama?"

I nodded.

He took in a breath. "Ya sure? I been looking a long time now."

"Let's find out." I stepped off that porch and found I wasn't quite sure my feet could touch the ground, I felt so light.

Walked the whole way to Hattie's just a-praying. Please Lord, let him be her hickory baby. He kept asking me questions. Did she like cinnamon in her coffee? Did she sing about the bluebird in the morning? Did she sew?

Each yes, making it harder to walk. By the time I could see that cabin, I'd taken to running, old Abe keeping right up with me. Didn't even bother knocking, just busted right in.

Miss Rosie jumped, putting her sewing to her chest. Mr. Caleb stood, chisel ready for a fight. Hattie made for the bed. Seeing me, they all stopped. Seeing Abe, they stared. He'd been crying. In that cabin I could see he had the height on him, taller than the door he was.

And there must've been something about him 'cause Miss Rosie got outta that chair of hers and walked behind it. Stroking the back real sweetlike, she said, "You look like Earl." She had tears in her voice, but they hadn't reached her eyes yet. "You belong to my man, Earl?"

"Yessum, I do."

Miss Rosie's knees done give on her. Mr. Caleb had to catch her as she put her hand out to touch her son. To feel that boy she lost so long ago. Mr. Caleb helped her cross the room as Abe met her halfway, just a-crying and touching her hair and her lips.

"That you, Mama?"

She hugged him, drank in the smell of him, then threw her head back, shouting, "Hickory. He smells of hickory." Grabbing his face in her hands, she say, "You my Abraham."

"Yessum." He smiled so big you could've lit a room with them white teeth.

She set to hugging him and tugging him like she meant to test his sturdiness. Hattie just stood there a-staring, Caleb shaking his head, saying, "Well, I'll be."

Miss Rosie stepped back and wiped her eyes. "Now, Abraham. What become of your brothers, your papa?"

Abraham bowed his head. "Jacob, he went north. Got him a ride on the railroad about seven years ago. Ain't heard tell of Isaac in about two years now. He got sold on."

"We find 'em, honey." She rubbed his cheek. "We found you, didn't we?" She laughed and looked at me, the happy going down to the pit of her soul. "Earl?"

"I'm sorry, Mama. Poppy gone. A fever took him."

Miss Rosie's faced dropped into sorrow. "Quick or slow?"

"He went quick, Mama. Fever too high for him to know it."

"May the Good Lord keep him." Miss Rosie touched her heart, then smiled real big with a laugh. "Long as he give me back my boy!"

They hugged for the longest time, then Miss Rosie put out supper and Abraham told us about his new job working the docks in Biloxi. Every now and again, I felt like leaving, this being a family time and all, but Miss Rosie, she put her hand over mine and say, "Stay, Stella. I want you to see my Abraham. Want everyone to see my Abraham." Even took him round to the sharecropping cabins on the Hendersen's place, introducing him around to all the folks they'd known for years.

Even with the happiness that filled those little cabins, I could still see them bare walls and those dirt floors and those holes for windows. No fireplace, no real comforts, places looked worse than the cabins folk'd come from. But they had places of their own and with all that laughter and story filling them up, I could almost forget where I sat.

That is, until I had to head home and found the front door hanging open and walked in to find Mr. Dooley near about passed out at the dining room table. Then, when I sat down, I knew I'd taken a seat in the little old hell that Richardson had made.

Cracking

"Do forgive me, Miss Reid." Even with his clothes all wrinkled and his eyes all red, Mr. Dooley tried to sit up straight and, as he would say, "look proper." He fumbled to button up his cuffs. "A gentleman never drinks to excess." The tone in his voice said he quoted his father again. "But that's quite the problem here, isn't it? I'm not a gentleman."

Everything about the man said gentleman. His clothes. The way he talked. How he ate his food, napkin on his knee, elbows off the table, nibbling away like a little rabbit.

He sighed. "It appears I've done it again. Tried to follow my own road only to end up in an alley with no way out."

I didn't follow him there, but since he was mostly talking to himself already, I figured he'd explain.

"You see," he leaned in close and I could smell my granddaddy's scotch on his breath. "My father has forever told me I haven't the initiative nor the stamina to make my own way in this world. Not like you." He held his glass up to me. "No, you, my dear, have the stamina of an Amazon."

I didn't know stamina from a stamen, but I figured he meant something good by it.

"I mean, how many grown men could accomplish what you've done here? Arranged a business deal to keep a stake in your family plantation. Keeping logs. Fighting fires."

"Wasn't alone."

"Hardly, but I can see the way these people respect you. And forgive me, dear, but you're barely older than a child and you have more respect in this world than I'll ever have."

"You ain't dead yet."

He spurted out a laugh. "Well, thank you for that inspiring point. But I might as well be, because I've had to summon the judge."

"The judge?"

He threw his head back and got all uppity in his voice. "Judge Conrad Dooley senior." Letting his head loll forward, he added in a slur, "My father."

A judge? Maybe he could put some sense into them courts. Talk judge talk to get one of them men to sign off on our deed and rule on that contract holding Hattie. "You think he'll make a difference?"

"My father has senators who do his bidding. No one says 'no' to Conrad Dooley senior. Why do you think I'm here?"

I hadn't a clue.

"I'm here"—he took a swig—"because there wasn't a courtroom in Massachusetts that hadn't heard of my father, didn't fear what he'd do if they crossed me or treated me badly because of what he'd already done to them. I walked in his shadow every day of my life. Did me no good to move to New York or Philadelphia. The further south I traveled, the greater his fame and influence became.

"Finally, I just decided the only way to get out from under his shadow would be to leave the law altogether. So here I am!" He threw up his hands and laughed.

Felt right sorry for him. Here I spent my days longing for my daddy to be with me and he just wanted to be free of his. Didn't seem right atall.

"And now, not only has the law followed me here, but so has the legend of my father. The only judge who is willing to hear a word I have to say is a man who knows my father from law school. Can you believe it? All this way and I meet up with one of father's old chums. Won't talk to me unless my father's present." Mr. Dooley took a quick drink, then shook his head.

As the clock struck midnight, he leaned forward to whisper, "Some independence, eh? Haven't been here much over a month and I had to call for my daddy."

Something in what he said lit a match inside my head, a glowing idea that I couldn't quite put a finger on.

"Happy Independence Day!" he shouted into the air.

Midnight on July third. That made it Independence Day. Fourth of July, 1866. I could see Daddy, clear as if he sat there across from me, raising a glass to independence. "You wait, Stella. You just wait, by this day next year, we'll be celebrating a real independence day. A day when every man can walk free in this country. Free as the Good Lord meant for them to be. *Wha-hoo!*"

Daddy'd said that not two weeks before he died in July of 1864. Just stung me raw to know he never did see the freedom come to the Natchez district. Sure, he saw the colored folks who refused to work or run off to join the Union once the war started. Even saw all the people who headed north as the Yankees came south. But he never did see it become the law of the land that no man could own another. And I sat there hoping he could see it all from heaven.

Remembering Daddy's words again made me think real hard. 7-4-65. That's the date he thought everyone would remember for its true freedom. And he never even saw the end of the war to know that'd be the first Fourth of July thereafter. Seemed like my daddy had prophesized.

I spun out of my chair and hightailed it down those stairs so fast, I don't remember going down them. All I do recall is spinning that safe lock so fast I lost count. Had to start over.

7. Click.

Oh, please, dear Lord.

4. Around again. 4. Click.

How sweet the sound.

"Miss Reid?" Heard Mr. Dooley behind me, but I didn't pay him no mind, just kept spinning.

65. Clunk.

That handle turned. That door opened. I'd gotten in!

To smell nothing but metal and dust. A big old empty safe.

Dropped to the floor and just stared into that thing.

"So you do have the combination, then?" Mr. Dooley dropped onto the bed. "Good. I have a few things I'd like to put in there."

So much for independence. Here I thought I'd crack that safe and find just what we needed. But right about then, I didn't know what that could be.

Daddy should've left me something in there. Any old thing to make all that trying worthwhile. I practically climbed into the thing to feel around. What with all his hidden stashes of money, I wouldn't put it past Daddy to put him a secret door even in a safe.

Ouch! I'd cut myself. Sucking on my bleeding finger, I felt like a fool until I realized there had to be a metal edge to be cutting myself. Going real slow, I went back to the same spot and sure enough, right there in the back, under the shelf, Daddy had worked in a little door.

"Hand me a letter opener, Mr. Dooley." I held my hand out behind me, but nothing happened.

Checking, I saw that he'd fallen asleep. A lot of help he turned out to be. I got up to get the letter opener, then went at that little door with a prying sense of adventure. And sure enough, I popped that thing open and out fell a key and a letter.

Daddy never was one for writing, so he kept it short. "To my Gayle Anne and my Stella Evelyne, I leave everything I am to you. Love, Sebastian."

Daddy was a key? Not hardly, but that's what he left us. A key to something. But what? Didn't have no other safes. No lockboxes. Then again, I never knew my room door had a lock, so I set to finding other doors, I'd never thought to lock. Went from room to room in the house, trying everything—drawers, cabinets, even checked for drawers within drawers, false backs, hidden doors. I done touched every single piece of wood and glass in that whole place before Mr. Dooley came staggering into bed.

"Please do fetch me a pitcher of water, dear. I need lots of it if I hope to be human come morning."

I headed down to the pump without even thinking. Wasn't till I got to the top of the stairs before I heard her. Mama begging for water from her room, her voice so low and scratchy she sounded like she'd already been buried in the earth. That pitcher got stone heavy, them steps twice as tall.

"Please, baby, just a sip. One little sip."

I could see Mama's face, her bleeding lips, the hair clinging to her yellow skin.

The memory of it grew too strong. I dropped that vase, water splashing everywhere when it broke. I didn't want that water touching me, giving me what she couldn't have.

Jumped out of the way, but lost my balance, felt the lung-sweeping gush of a fall backward, heard that glass break again, a foot slide in the water, felt a grip on my dress, then a rip, another step, an arm under my back, and I crashed into the side of the stairwell, Mr. Dooley pulling up and over at the same time, his arm nearly over his head as he gripped the railing behind him.

Dropping to the stair with me in his lap, he hugged me hard. "Dear heavens."

Putting a hand to each of my ears, he pulled my face back to have a look. "What on earth happened?"

"My mama died of yellow fever."

"And?" he whispered.

"They wouldn't give her any water." I cried right there in that strange man's lap. Cried till I didn't have no tears left, him rocking me, and cooing, combing my hair back, near about everything my daddy would've done if he'd been there. Funny how close you can feel to a stranger when he soothes your heart like that.

When I'd cried myself out, I sat up and asked, "You want that water now?"

He pulled at his wet shirt. "I think I've had enough, thank you."

I smiled.

Giving me a gentle push toward the top of the stairs, he said, "Better try to get some rest, Miss Stella."

He gave my hand a squeeze as I got up to go. And for the first time, I crawled into that bed in that big old house and felt a little like I might be at home.

Fathers

Mr. Dooley went to get his father at the train station in Natchez. I spent the morning helping Mrs. Wynston fix the place up. With the hurry of it all pushing me along, I found I could actually put a hand into cleaning without making a mess. My mama had taught me a thing or two after all. I polished up the furniture, shook the rugs out over the veranda, even put fresh flowers in each room. Now, I still don't have the touch to make a mirror look like anything more than a murky pond, but the cleaning, not that I'd let a living soul know, gave me a bit of peace with a little memory swirled in. Like Mama might be watching. Even thought I caught a glimpse of her in the rush of drapes when the wind took them or in a streak of sunlight that crossed my path as I turned a corner, each time she looked at me just a-smiling. Felt good to have her with me.

Daddy came along too. His key in my pocket. His words echoing in my head, "I give all of myself to you." Just what could he have left behind? They'd killed him before he could sign any deed. And Mama never found Granddaddy's will neither. He used to keep it with his lawyer who'd died not two months before

Daddy in a fire that took him and all his papers. With all of the fires of late, I began to wonder if Richardson and his lot had set that one too. Back then, they blamed a lamp the lawyer left lit on his desk, but I didn't buy that lie no more.

What I needed to know right then was what Daddy had hidden away for me to find. Had to be something of his, but what? Man never kept much for himself, always giving to other people. Never kept a diary, except the log, or even sat for a picture. I had no idea.

And I had no more time to look because Big Daddy Dooley came a-bursting in, just a-yelling. "This place is a shambles, Conrad. Just a shambles. Scorch marks on your house, people living in the outbuildings like animals."

"But we've got fine cotton growing in the fields, Father. A bumper crop, they're saying." Mr. Dooley sounded all squeaky and scared.

I stood on the upstairs landing looking down at a bull of a man charging through the house, with Mr. Dooley rushing to keep up. That big old man turned on his son, asking, "And have you seen the price of cotton this year? Practically pennies. You know, son, I really do wish you had consulted me before buying this place. I would've told you . . ."

Mr. Dooley stopped. "You would have told me what to do."

"Why, of course I would have."

"I can make my own decisions, Father."

"Not very wise ones, I'd wager."

"I didn't bring you here for your advice, father."

"No, you wanted to trade on my influence again. Well, I should expect something in return."

"Like what? I wasn't aware that I'd hired you. Here I thought you'd come to help a son in need."

"What my son needs is a good head on his shoulders. Not a mind full of crazy schemes!"

"How do," I said from the stairs, hoping to head off the battle I seen brewing in my front hall. When they kept shouting, I yelled all the louder. "How do!"

"My good heavens." That old man spun around and grabbed his chest like I'd done bit him in the backside. "Who is she?"

Mr. Dooley had to swallow a laugh before stepping up to offer his hand to me. I did my best imitation of Mama and took his hand and walked the rest of the way down, him saying, "This is Miss Stella Reid, the lady of the house."

"Lady? She sounded like a bullfrog."

"Father."

He stared at me like I was a bullfrog in a dress. "I've never heard a woman yell like that."

Mr. Dooley led the way into the sitting room and we all sat down. I couldn't help like feeling I sat on a pin cushion, that settee had been that overstuffed.

"You've also never seen one fight a fire or dig a ditch or keep books, but this one does. And she can also do a fair turn on the piano. That is, if you're interested in hearing 'Camptown Races.'"

My favorite.

"But who is she?" Big Daddy Dooley asked as Mrs. Wynston came in with iced tea.

"The daughter of the last owners. They've passed on, but she's been holding things together in their absence quite well."

"A young woman?"

"That's right."

Big Daddy Dooley took tea from Mrs. Wynston, then pointed at me with his glass. "*She's* the savvy business partner you wrote to me about?"

I didn't like the way he took that tea without even looking at Mrs. Wynston, not to mention forgetting to thank her. Not Mr. Dooley. He even smiled when he thanked her. Then he handed his father my log. "Look at this, Father, she's kept it all herself."

I felt like dumping it on the floor with his tea, so he'd look at Mrs. Wynston, see the person who'd served him, would cook his meals, turn down his bed, and empty his chamber pot.

But he dove into that book like a starving man into a good meal. "Impressive. My, my . . ." He used a long string of them kind of words, then looked at me like I'd just told him a lie. "You did all of this yourself?"

Should I have written it in my own blood to prove I'd done it?

"Yes, sir."

Saw Mrs. Wynston sweeping the front hall of all the dirt they'd tracked in. I rushed over to pull her into the doorway. "And I'd like you to meet Mrs. Casadine Wynston. Keeper of this here house." She fussed and blushed.

Big Daddy Dooley got that look of *Oh my, what have I missed?*, then stood up and gave her a little bow. "Mrs. Wynston." Looking around, he added, "You keep a fine home."

Now, that I could abide by. A man who saw a woman's value— whether she cleaned, hoed, or yelled.

"Thank you, sir." She gave me a little bit of nudge, then turned away. "And I better get back to it."

Stretching his back, that old man said, "You know, Conrad, there may be a bit more here than meets the eye."

Mr. Dooley blinked at me, then ushered his father into the hallway. "Well, let me just show you how much more."

"Miss Stella." Mr. Vinson came in the back door as they went out the front. Using a table to unroll the plans he'd brought, he asked, "Who that?"

"Mr. Dooley's father."

"He looking to work here too?"

I shook my head. Could see Mr. Vinson needed more information, so I said, "He's a judge, come to help with the deed."

"Do tell. That'd be mighty fine."

I tapped the paper, seeing he intended to show me plans. Thought he'd brought me sketches for the new cabins—after all, he and Daddy had designed and built every new building on the place. But the plans he'd brought showed a building way too big to be a cabin. We didn't have enough wood for cabins let alone big old buildings like the ones he'd drawn.

"Thought we could save wood and money by building us bigger cabins that four families can live in. One roof. Four rooms. Could even do one chimney with a fireplace big enough to have a hearth on four sides."

Such a place looked a whole lot better than an empty horse stall or any other place the folks'd been sleeping for the last month, but I didn't see any of them taking to the idea of having to share their cabins after losing such fine ones. Then again, the word "share" had me thinking on them awful places sharecroppers been living in. The big cabins might look good after all that.

"Worth a vote."

He slapped the table. "Sure enough is!" He started rolling up his plan. "Think I should track down Mr. Dooley?"

"I'd wait for the meeting. He'll be mighty tied up with his daddy."

"And how about you?" He tapped my shoulder with the plans. "How you holding up, Miss Stella? You looking a bit pale again."

Well, I'd brought Miss Rosie her Abraham, found out Mr. Dooley cared a good deal more than he let on, and felt kind of to home in the old place. All in all, I felt pretty good, especially if Big Daddy Dooley could do something about our legal troubles.

"Things are good."

"Careful now." Mr. Vinson smiled. "You know what they say. . . ."

"This too shall pass." We said it together, both of us laughing.

Most of the time we said that to keep each other laughing or remembering Daddy, but this time I couldn't help but think, couldn't good times pass into better times? Does it always have to go from good to bad?

Well, if the meeting that night would be any indication, weren't no better times on the horizon. Big Daddy Dooley put on his bull act again and nearly tore the whole place up, saying business meetings are no place for prayer, Mr. Vinson's plans would build nothing but fire hazards, and he didn't see no call for allowing women to vote. "They can't vote for our country, there's no reason for them to vote on our business!" he shouted. So much for seeing a woman's worth.

Folks just stared at him, not sure if they should debate him or just laugh at him, he was so downright disagreeable, and frankly kind of funny, in his mixed-up ideas. I couldn't even look at him. Had to keep my eyes on the walls to keep from laughing.

By the time they called the vote for the cabin plans, I believe I had counted every knothole in the place. Felt like my eyes had gone a little funny 'cause I couldn't keep my eyes off them. When the vote on Mr. Vinson's plans carried, Big Daddy Dooley started to have him a yelling fit, so Mr. Dooley shooed him out the door. Peeked his head in to apologize, then disappeared. That's when the laughter started, and the talking, everyone wondering just what that big old bag of wind could be doing for us.

Heard someone say, "What you think, Miss Stella?"

But I had something pulling me into those knotholes. Dark wood, almost black under the stain, like a keyhole—a whole mess of keyholes just staring at me, empty and waiting.

Heard God ask as clear as a bird on a branch, *Where would he keep his dream?*

"Not in no house, that's for sure." I said it out loud and everybody stared at me, but I didn't care. I'd just looked in the house for Daddy's little treasure, but why would he've kept it there? Place didn't mean a thing to him. I had a whole plantation to search. Didn't feel like telling no one, so I started in the stables while the folks were away.

Heard some children playing over in the blacksmith shop, metal swinging with a whine with their laughter echoing it. Remembered Mr. Beeman working in there, the whoosh of his bellows keeping harmony with the clang of his hammer.

Bury it where's folks are too afraid to find it.

And what did Daddy have that scared people? Seeing the horses' names on the stalls, I remembered Zephyr, that old stallion Daddy'd had, so mean and ornery Mama sold that thing before they buried Daddy. He loved it. Swore he'd break it so's I could ride him. Probably would have too, if he'd had the time.

Miss Maggie and Mr. Zachariah, the stablemaster, called his stall home these days. Their older children musta been off playing because the place looked empty when I opened the door. Zachariah done hung their family name over Zephyr's. Looked mighty nice.

Felt wrong to go digging through their things, but I had to know. Being real careful, I checked every wall, even started rolling up their beds until their daughter Zella come back. "You lose something, Miss Stella?"

"Think my daddy left me something."

"In here?" asked her brother Timothy, coming around his sister.

I nodded.

"Think it's under here?" He threw back a blanket to show me a hunk a' cement, the kind Daddy used to hold up posts and pour down floors. But this piece weren't no bigger than my log book and it didn't even touch the side of the stall. What it did have was a couple of footprints, big as you please. Would Daddy have buried it under that? Or inside it?

"Maybe," I said.

"I'll get us a shovel." Timothy went running.

"Make that two," I yelled back.

We set to digging and as the folks came back the story spread, Mr. Zachariah taking over for Timothy and us getting deeper and deeper as the crowd got thicker and thicker. I got down to scrape away the dirt and check how deep we'd gone and see if I could . . . "I feel the bottom!"

"She feels the bottom!" someone shouted in the throughway and the word spread through the crowd, folks shouting, "What's down there?" and the like.

"It's metal!" I yelled back. Daddy done put a lockbox in cement.

"We be needing rope." Mr. Zachariah ran off for a rope and came back with that and a horse, Old Valiant, in fact. "He's better at pulling." He patted Valiant's flank. Folks laughed, but Mr. Zachariah had called it right. When we tied that rope off on the old boy's harness, Valiant done pulled that block out like it wasn't nothing but a basket of laundry.

"What's inside?" yelled the children as they gathered around.

But Mr. Harris, the carpenter, and Mr. Zachariah shooed them away, Mr. Harris saying, "Girl needs to look at it her own self."

"We'll haul it over to the office for you, Miss Stella."

"Thank you," I said, heading out, my hands just itching to see inside that box.

Hattie waited on the stoop when I got there. Seeing me, she done hug me till I couldn't breathe. "Thank you, thank you, thank you. May the Lord keep thanking you till the end of heaven."

I laughed as she let go. "All I did was write a letter or two."

"I don't care what you did. You give my mama back her heart. She smiling and laughing and singing. I ain't seen her this happy in my whole life."

"That's wonderful." True tell, I felt the happy of it clean down to the soles of my feet.

"It sure is." She dropped down onto the stoop and stretched in the goodness of it all. "And that Abraham, he's a fine man. He taking to the woodworking my daddy's showing him like he was born to it." She set to pulling at the stuffing in the hole in her shoe. A true tell that she didn't altogether like having her a brother.

"Ain't fair he won't show you."

"That's what I said. Said, 'Look at Stella. Ain't no boy thing she don't do. Why can't I work wood?'"

"What Mr. Caleb say to that?"

Hattie rolled her eyes. "'You ain't Stella.'"

I laughed, sitting down next to her. "And I bet your mama glad for that, too."

She gave me a shove, then whispered, "Said I should be glad to be the fine girl the Good Lord made me."

"See there. Now me, I don't like nothing about being no girl."

"Ya don't say?" Hattie gave me her big-eyed stare and we both laughed, then Mr. Harris and Mr. Zachariah came around the corner with a little wagon Mr. Caleb had made for Timothy, that big old hunk near about burying the wheels in the dirt.

"What's that?" Hattie asked as they unloaded it.

"You want for us to bring this inside?" asked Mr. Zacariah.

I shook my head.

Mr. Harris looked just about ready to stay for a look-see, but Mr. Zachariah gave him a nudge. They walked off with the wagon, but Hattie near about swallowed the thing, she got so close.

"Whose footprints are those?" she asked.

In all the digging, I'd had my mind on getting it free, didn't even look at them prints much. "Get the lantern."

Hattie grabbed the lantern off the hook by the office door, then brought it up close.

Saw the star right off. Daddy. We'd buried him in those boots. I traced the star with my finger.

"Okay," said Hattie, knowing what that meant. "But what about this one?" She pointed to the other shoe, facing Daddy's and all smeared up on the side, with nothing but muck next to it, like they might've been fighting. I held my breath. Daddy died just feet from the stable door. Zephyr had him a stall on the very end. Had Daddy fought his killer over that block?

Hattie saw the fear in my face. She sighed, then turned the block in the dirt. "Let's have a look at what he left."

I yanked that key out, then I saw the lock. The cement had dripped right over it. Couldn't unlock that thing if I had a pick, and I mean a coal pick.

Hattie just pulled herself back then gave that old box a good kick. Didn't do nothing but dent it. Still, something about that looked just right. I kicked it too. Then she did. Then I did. Both of us laughing and feeling pretty good about letting that box have the works.

And *bouck!* It popped open. Coins and paper fell out.

"Money!" Hattie yelled, collecting up the coins.

I took up the papers, afraid to look. A funny kind of book fell out first. A little bound-up book no bigger than my hand, each page a receipt with half of it torn away, but every single one of them signed by Hendersen and Markham, last one saying, "Paid in full." Daddy's payment book. Kissed that thing and put it over my heart to slow it down. Markham couldn't go claiming interest due. Taking Oak Grove weren't legal after all. Take that, you thieving fool.

Then I saw a piece of Daddy's letter-writing paper and had a look. Another letter to me and Mama. His "double rose," as he called us. Letter said, "I give you all that I am, but knowing your hearts, I've given it to the folks as well."

My fingers turned to steam as I tried to open the other papers all stiff and gray and long, handwriting loopy and fancy like none I'd ever seen, but sure as God watches from heaven, Daddy'd done left us not just a will, but a deed. A deed to Oak Grove written down to Mrs. Gayle Anne Reid, wife, Miss Stella Evelyne Reid, daughter, Mr. Gabriel Vinson, foreman, and the names went on for two pages. Daddy done give it to us all!

I got to my feet, bent myself way back to put my chest up to the moon. "Thank you, Daddy." He done give us Oak Grove after all. And died doing it. "Thank you."

Walking the Right Road

I ran for the meeting house and rang that bell until my ears nearly bled, folks coming a-running, but I didn't say a word one. Just waited for everyone to come. Mr. Dooley and his daddy came charging along in their fancy robes and slippers.

"What is all this?" asked Big Daddy Dooley, looking all puffy-eyed and sleepy.

But he had to wait like the rest of them until the foreman, Mr. Vinson say, "We all here, Miss Stella."

I ran in, jumped on Daddy's chair and threw my arm up, deed in hand. "He did it. Daddy kept his promise!"

Folks looked all nervous, shifting and passing glances.

"Did what, Miss Stella?" asked Old Jasper.

Mr. Vinson shook his head, but I could almost hear the prayer leaving his lips.

"He deeded Oak Grove to us all. Every last one of us."

That roof took a beating with all the hooting and hollering and stomping going on in that building. I just did my dance from Daddy's chair, keeping that deed close to my heart. Could've danced till the day I died. But folks came up to have them a look and find their names. Some traced their names. Some kissed the deed. Some put it to their hearts. Others prayed over it.

I just wanted to kiss my daddy to thank him for all he done for us. But Pastor Rallsom did that for us, thanking Daddy and the Good Lord who protected him long enough to get it done.

As Mr. Vinson took his look, he said, "Your daddy must've had two deeds drawn up to try and fool Richardson."

"He did fool him." I laughed, but it stung knowing that man could still be the one who took Daddy's life.

"He sure enough did." Mr. Vinson smiled, but I noticed something I hadn't before.

We had people missing, and not just those troublemakers like Lennox and Carter who should've been there to know they never did speak true of my daddy, but I couldn't find Mr. Dooley anywhere.

"You seen Mr. Dooley?" I asked Mrs. Wynston. That woman never missed a thing.

"He left with his daddy."

So I went to find him.

The two them had set to packing, Big Daddy in his room calling his son every kind of idiot. And Mr. Dooley in Granddaddy's room calling himself the fool.

"Where you going?" I asked Mr. Dooley.

He laughed. "Possession may be nine-tenths of the law, Miss Reid." He pointed at the deed in my hand. "But that's the tenth that counts."

"What about all your money?"

"I'll be visiting Mr. Markham in the morning to see about that, but even with that payment book and the deed, I wager it'll take years before I see a dime."

Watching him throw clothes in that suitcase all flustered, felt kind of hollow. Didn't know what to say so I asked the Lord for a little help and He said, *I don't send gifts I expect to be returned.*

God had sent Mr. Dooley to Oak Grove for a reason and by the sounds of things that reason hadn't ended just 'cause I found the deed, so I said, "Well, we could use that money."

"We?"

"Got cabins to build, belts need replacing, cotton to take up to Natchez 'cause won't a boat captain on the river go against a powerful man like Richardson to take it for us. Unless you think you got enough for a boat?"

"Pardon?"

Knew he just needed a little time to let that sink in, so I waited.

"What is she going on about, Conrad?" Big Daddy Dooley asked from the hall.

Mr. Dooley had a sly kind of smile, when he asked, "Are you suggesting a partnership, Miss Reid?"

I nodded. "With all them things, Richardson couldn't stop us."

"That is, if we can get the funds out of the bank."

I waved the deed. "How could they sell what they didn't have no right to own?"

And that meant Mr. Vinson had a right to the money they paid for the fallow land as well. Why, they'd have cash money to buy more land come tax time. So would Mr. Dooley and I. Why, we might could double Oak Grove in size. Wouldn't that be a turnaround fit for just desserts?

"So true, my dear. So true."

"What is she talking about?"

"Father, I'm back in the planting business."

He offered me a hand and we shook on it. Even did us a bit of a jig right there, that being the first time I learned Dooley to be an Irish name. But with Mr. Dooley staying on, I figured I'd learn a good deal more about other cultures.

Then again, we hadn't exactly cleared the forest just yet.

First stop, the next morning, the bank and Mr. Markham. Man put up a fuss and a holler, didn't even back down when Big Daddy Dooley, the judge himself, started blustering.

Finally, the young Mr. Dooley took my bullfrog approach and yelled louder than anybody else, "Is this a deed or isn't it!"

Mr. Markham jumped and covered his heart, which had to be beating faster than a racehorse's right about then.

"Well?" Mr. Dooley shook the deed.

"I suppose it is, but I'd rather wait for Mr. Richardson."

"Well, was it Richardson or was it you who signed this payment book, 'Paid in Full'?" He tapped the page over Markham's signature.

"That would've been me, sir."

"Did Richardson auction the land?"

"No, sir."

"Then give us the money!"

That yell sent Mr. Markham scurrying like we'd done set fire to his britches. He came back all sweating and fumbly. "We may not have every dime today, but I can be sure to give you a promissory note for the rest."

"Are you willing to take a note from this man, Mr. Vinson?"

Mr. Vinson looked like he done swallowed a frog. He'd never

even been allowed to step foot in that bank before, let alone have a chance to demand his money, but he knew his rights and he stood up for them. "I'll take the cash."

"All right, then." Mr. Dooley slapped the counter and sent Mr. Markham to counting. Mr. Vinson counted right along with him, smoothed that money out fine and tucked it away. I prayed for the Lord to keep him safe until he could find a proper place for that money.

Then Mr. Dooley creased his brow and said, "I will have two thousand nine hundred and fifty-seven dollars. You can put the rest in my account."

"You trust *him*?" I whispered.

"More than I trust carrying this kind of money with Richardson around."

He had a point there.

Markham counted out the money and as he did, I realized the number added up to just what I'd given Dooley for a stake in Oak Grove. What did he have in mind?

"Now, will you be stuffing this back into hidey-holes around the place, or shall we start an account for your college education?"

"You're sending me to college?"

"With your drawing talent and that growing need to learn of yours, I doubt I'll have much to say on the matter come time for you to attend."

Well, I didn't much like the idea of leaving Oak Grove, but that money might come in handy later on, so I agreed to open an account, but in the bank in Natchez. Didn't want that Markham touching anything I owned.

We walked out a that bank with Mr. Vinson holding his money, me holding mine, and Mr. Dooley looking right proud. But not his daddy. No, his daddy went on about fools and their money, but sounded more like he'd gone to talking about himself to me.

Before we so much as stepped off the boardwalk, Miss Shaw came shuffling up to us, all dusty and *see-here*. "Mr. Dooley, Miss Mertle Seeton would like to see you."

"She would?" Mr. Dooley squinted. Probably felt the same tight squeeze around his heart I did, wondering what that woman could be wanting of us now. Would she really ask for her money back if she knew we meant to turn Oak Grove over to the people who worked it?

Miss Shaw just smiled at Mr. Dooley like he done sprouted wings or something, saying, "She's heard about the change of affairs over at the Reid place and would like to discuss it with you as a concerned party."

Concerned party? What is she doing? Sitting over there in a fancy hat with a bunch of cakes and pies? Why can't people just say what they mean?

"Of course, I would be delighted." Mr. Dooley nodded, but Big Daddy just barked, "Who is this Seeton woman?"

Miss Shaw near about jumped out of her bloomers for the startlement of it. Had to chew back a laugh, and I could've sworn I seen Mr. Vinson covering his mouth to hide a smile.

"No worries, Father. It'll just take but a minute. Why don't you and the others make ready for our trip to the courthouse. Stella and I will be along directly."

Oh, bother, I had to go too.

Cousin Mertle waited for us in the parlor, all stiff and proper.

She offered Mr. Dooley her hand, saying "Mr. Dooley" as he kissed it.

I didn't like the stiff, *I-need-to-have-a-word-with-you* sound in her voice.

"I must be frank. The recent turn of events has me worried for Stella's safety. That fire and . . ." She shivered. "I won't have her life at risk, Mr. Dooley."

Either her eyes had started to water from age or Miss Mertle was fixing to cry. That old woman had more surprises in her than a cornered bear.

Mr. Dooley's face softened, his eyes gaining the weight of respect as he looked at her. "Indeed, madam. I must admit my ignorance of the way of things down here has cost too much already, but I plan to see to it that the deed Mr. Reid had drawn up is properly filed so there can be no more disputes over the ownership of Oak Grove."

"So, you'll be staying on."

"Yes." He smiled. "It appears that Miss Reid favors me as a tutor and a business partner."

Cousin Mertle shook her head. "I am getting too old for these strange affairs. I knew that Sebastian Reid would be making things difficult the moment I laid eyes on him. Apart from breathing, he never did a straight and proper thing in his entire life."

That had me on my feet and talking before I felt my tongue leave my mouth. "Daddy was a fine man."

Mr. Dooley grabbed my arm to quiet me, probably fixing to go on about respecting my elders and such.

"Now, Stella." Miss Mertle patted my hand. "Have pity on an old woman. Your father may have had peculiarities about him, but that doesn't mean I didn't respect him from a distance."

Dear Lord, tell me what she's saying now. I seen her smile and then turn toward the window. The Lord showed me all them folks walking down the street, acting all fancy and such. Realized she meant she could admire Daddy just as long as other folks thought she preferred things properlike. Well, I guess I couldn't blame her too much. I mean, she was old. Changing this late in life might be bad for her health.

"Yes, ma'am," I said, sitting down.

She patted my knee. "I just wanted to be sure Mr. Dooley would continue in his duties and give me his oath that you'll be safe."

Mr. Dooley stood up proud. "I'd consider it an honor."

"You consider yourself honor-bound and we have us an agreement."

She offered her hand. They shook. And we walked out, me shaking my head and Mr. Dooley laughing. I scowled at him.

"Stella, my dear, you must remember, not every woman goes straight after what she wants. On occasion, they use a bit of diplomacy and secrecy."

"Come again?"

"While you'd grab a problem by the throat, she'd be more inclined to feed it something sweet until it chokes. But you both reach the same goal in the end."

Mama always said, "Long as it's walked with the Lord, don't matter what road you choose to get to the right destination." So, I guess I had no call to be hard on Cousin Mertle for walking her own road as long as she let me walk on mine.

That'll Be the Judge

We met up with the others and headed off to the Adams County Courthouse with a tidy little stopover at the first bank in Natchez to offer accounts to colored folk. But that visit with Cousin Mertle had me thinking on how everyone takes their own path to solving problems—taking a torch to a building like Richardson and his goons, using sugarcoated talk while passing money off for a good cause like Cousin Mertle, or yelling and laying blame like Big Daddy Dooley—it all had me wondering just what young Mr. Dooley would do to sort things out at the courthouse.

And we had us a whole wagon full for that trip, with Miss Rosie, Mr. Caleb, Mr. Abraham and Hattie, then the Misters Dooley and Mr. Vinson, the lot of us singing the whole way. Well, Big Daddy Dooley wasn't much for songs, not even the Irish ones Mr. Dooley taught us.

After Mr. Dooley taught us one about leaving a rose on the grave of the one you love, Big Daddy asked all shameful, "Did you get that from your mother?", like his side of the family would never share such things.

Mr. Dooley, who'd probably heard such things all his life, squinted, then said, "No, your brother."

I smiled to see Big Daddy bluster and shake his head like he had a bad taste in his mouth, but Mr. Dooley just laughed.

Night had fallen before we reached the county seat and none of us were fool enough to try and find a hotel that would take the lot of us, so we found the Freedmen's Bureau and put up a row of tents with the other folks there.

Miss Rosie held her Abraham's hand all through dinner, knowing he'd gone to bureau after bureau looking for her. "We'll find them," she kept saying, meaning his brothers.

And I prayed she did.

But all Big Daddy did was complain about the food, the tents, the bugs. He didn't like one thing about our little adventure under the stars. "Why can't I just stay in a hotel?"

"Because you need to be here," said Mr. Dooley.

"What is that supposed to mean?"

"Weren't you the one who told me every man needs to know how the other half lives to truly defend him?"

Big Daddy clenched his jaw. "Do you remember every cotton-picking thing I say?"

"I'm afraid so."

"Well, start forgetting because I'm getting too old to do this kind of thing."

"Good night, Father."

"Good night!"

But he didn't sound none too good about the whole thing. And he looked far worse the next morning, all wrinkled clothes and stiff body. "I need a bath!" he yelled over breakfast.

So before heading to the courthouse, the Dooleys had a visit to the bathhouse and the rest of us had a look-see into the shops along the way. People stared us like we meant to rob the place, so we started walking, Hattie and her family having to look down every time a white person passed them by. Made me want to slap those people silly. Felt like grabbing the nearest person by the chin and forcing him to look at Miss Rosie—shake Mr. Caleb's hand. But like Mr. Dooley done told me, you can't change the world in one day, you got to do it one thing at a time. Wonder if he got that from his daddy?

Seeing the two of them walk up the courthouse steps, one a tall, thin shadow of the other, I could see Mr. Dooley's problem with his daddy. Folks noticed that big man first, gave him room, even nodded, with Mr. Dooley a step behind. But in my mind, that Mr. Dooley had his father whopped with his kindness, his patience, and when he dropped all that proper pooh, the respect he showed other folks. I'd hire him on any day.

Especially on that day. Mr. Bellingame, the county judge who went to law school with Big Daddy Dooley, agreed to see us. Even let us all in his office. He looked a mite uncomfortable, but he offered Miss Rosie a chair, before asking, "What can I do for you, Conrad?" Meaning Big Daddy.

"It's my son who wishes to talk to you." Big Daddy Dooley even stepped behind his son to let him make his point.

"I'll start plainly, Judge Bellingame." He put one hand on Miss Rosie's shoulder and one on Mr. Caleb's with Hattie standing between them. "A Mr. Lars Hendersen of Helensburg has claimed that this young lady is an orphan in need of his

238

protection under a labor contract that makes her his ward. Yet these are the parents of this very girl, who are in fact married and have been for nineteen years. And both of them are gainfully employed. He as a carpenter, she as a seamstress."

"They have proof of employment?" The judge asked, sitting forward in his chair, his elbow on the desk, his hand out, waiting for the proof.

"Hendersen refuses to provide documentation to that fact."

"Well, I . . ." The judge started talking, but Mr. Caleb took a step forward, saying, "Beg your pardon, sir, but I been making furniture on the Henderson place since I been fourteen years old. Every stick of furniture in that house has my mark on it. And I have me here a letter from the Guardian Bank of Natchez showing I have me one thousand five hundred and twenty-three dollars saved up. And here's my order book, showing I got me twenty-one orders for furniture. Now I don't write so good, but I got me sketches of every piece I needs to make with they prices and the signature of the folks who ordered them." Mr. Caleb showed off the book, pointing to each item as he mentioned it. Man kept a better log than me.

"I see." The judge took the book with one hand and put his glasses on with the other.

"This be my log book." Miss Rosie stood and slipped it onto the desk. I could see from the writing that Hattie helped her put that together, but Miss Rosie didn't need to be staring at the floor like she did. Weren't no one that worked as hard as she, and it wouldn't be no time before she could write as good as anyone in the room if they'd just give her some peace of mind and the rights to her children back.

Mr. Vinson stood up. "I can bear witness, sir. I've known these two fine people since they's first married."

The judge just kept nodding. "That's fine. That's fine." Looking at Dooley, he said, "Did you have a copy of this contract?"

"Hendersen refused to offer a copy, as did the bureau in Helensburg, but I do have the correspondence regarding the contract that went among the agent, Mr. Hendersen, and the supervisor for that bureau, a Colonel Shepard."

"Well, this Hendersen won't be hiding behind his lack of cooperation. This girl is clearly no orphan in need of aid. Any contract written on those grounds is null and void and I will write a letter to all parties testifying to that fact."

"You will?" Mr. Caleb asked.

"Certainly." He folded up the letters and set them on his desk. He started to hand back the log books, but Miss Rosie took up his free hand and started shaking it so hard he nearly dropped them.

"Thank you, sir. Thank you so much."

"Yes, yes. You're welcome." He pulled his hand back, then offered the log books to Mr. Caleb, who grabbed the free hand and gave it a quick shake, saying, "Mighty grateful, sir."

The judge nodded.

As Hattie and her folks took to hugging, Abraham joining in, Mr. Dooley said, "We're only in town for another night, Judge Bellingame. Could you see your way clear to writing up a letter addressed to the young lady's parents that they could take with them? We could come round to pick it up tomorrow."

The judge frowned, but said, "That'd be fine." He sighed, then asked, "What last name do you folks go by?"

"Woodman," Mr. Caleb said. First I'd heard they'd picked a last name, but it was a good one for them to have, that's for sure.

At the door, Mr. Dooley said, "Oh, I have one more issue to address, Judge Bellingame."

"What's that?"

"Would you be so kind as to verify that this deed has been filed properly for my client, Miss Reid."

Having him say my name froze me up, right there.

"Is that why she's with you?"

"Yes, sir."

"All right, give me the deed. Come back tomorrow morning. I'll have your papers ready for you then."

"Thank you, sir." Out we went, Miss Rosie and Mr. Caleb so happy they practically danced, Big Daddy complaining about another night sleeping with bugs. Mr. Dooley acting all proud.

Feeling a little stuck inside, I asked, "What if he knows Richardson and tears up that deed?"

"He wouldn't dare!" barked Big Daddy from up ahead.

"There you have it. And unlike most big dogs," said Mr. Dooley as he nodded to his father, "*he* has a rather nasty bite."

"Are you calling me a dog?"

"No, Father, of course not."

Hattie and I fell a little behind, so we could laugh without being heard. Mr. Dooley looked over his shoulder and made a dog face, pretending to bark. That made us laugh all the harder. That Mr. Dooley had a bit of the devilment in him. All that proper talk probably came from his daddy, but I rather liked the side of him that did a jig and made dog faces after his daddy.

That night I couldn't sleep atall, what with the deed in the hands of that awful old judge and all. Miss Hattie Woodman sat up with me and we made wishes on lightning bugs.

"I wish we could find a place in Philadelphia with real honest-to-goodness beds."

I wanted to wish Hattie wouldn't be going to Philadelphia, but that would be wrong. She and her family had talked of going there since I don't know when.

Mr. Dooley had friends there, so he gave Mr. Caleb a few names to get them started, said they'd do fine—what with Mr. Caleb's work with furniture and Miss Rosie's fine hand at sewing. And there weren't no better bureaus than the ones up in Philadelphia—they'd be finding Miss Rosie's boys right quick.

But it'd be like losing my voice to have Hattie gone. She did most of my talking for me when other folks came around. Now I'd have to do it my own self. I hated even the idea of it.

"Might find somebody better at throwing peanuts."

That couldn't be too hard.

She gave me a shove. "I *heard* that!"

I put my arm over her shoulder and held on till morning.

Endings and Beginnings

By the time Hattie and I woke up, Miss Rosie and Mr. Caleb had them a fine letter saying Hattie be legally free and Mr. Dooley had our deed papers in his pocket. He let me have them straightaway. Hard to believe something so light could give me claim to something so big and true special.

Felt like my heart would just flatten out like a pressed flower under all that happiness, what with Hattie free and Miss Rosie's Abraham at her side. Not to mention the deed papers in my pocket. I near about got dizzy.

Only thing that could've brought me any closer to heaven right then would've been knowing that the man who killed my daddy and Mr. Beeman would be facing God's justice right soon.

As if his guilt just pulled him right to us, Richardson showed up. We had the wagon all packed up, Mr. Dooley even had his hand on the brake, when Richardson came storming up the boardwalk.

"You hold it right there!" He stopped by the side of the wagon. "You won't be going anywhere until I have my say with this judge you've bribed."

Big Daddy puffed out like an angry bird, yelling, "Bribed? I'll have you know I'm a federal judge, Mister."

"Father." Mr. Dooley put his hand on Big Daddy's arm, then he opened his mouth to speak.

Seeing that evil man lit a fire in me and sent me jumping over that wagon's side. The flames burst out a' me in blazing words. "You may walk and talk in this here world, but come the judgment, the Lord will strike you down. He knows what you done. Killed my daddy. Not to mention Mr. Beeman and Mr. Chance. Those souls will be weighing on you till this world ends and you'll be damned in the next. Don't go talking about no judge, because the one true judge be keeping an account on you. And you can't buy, bribe, or burn your way out of that book, Daniel Richardson, so you best turn yourself around and get to thinking real hard on what you'll be doing between now and your end."

That man never heard me say a sentence, let alone a paragraph, so I guess I'd stunned him into listening, if not with the words themselves than with the number of them. When Richardson tried to speak, Mr. Dooley stood up and said, "You heard the lady."

That poor damned Richardson turned around and walked off, knowing for sure certain that he could never scare us off our land. And by rights, it really was *our* land. And we rode in that wagon all the way back, singing and storytelling, me just aching to see Oak Grove.

Could almost taste the saucy bite of the pork Mr. Vinson would roast all day in God's good sun for the picnic we'd have to celebrate. A day of dancing and singing—Mr. Zachariah on the banjo, Mr. Garrett might even let me do a tune or two on the piano they'd take outside on boards that'd be the start of their make-for-a-day dance floor. Maybe I could get Mr. Dooley to show the folks a jig. But even if he said no, we'd be making grateful and happy from dawn to dark, with more laughing and food than a herd of elephants could bear.

Hearing the music in my head already, I closed my eyes to get a mind's-eye view of the cabins we'd build, making each one true special for every family on the plots they'd pick out to claim their own little piece of Oak Grove to have for always.

Could see us loading up the cotton for Natchez, wagon after wagon piled high with bales full to bursting, songs going up, and nobody to stand in our way.

Speaking of nobody, I couldn't wait to see Mr. Caleb and Mrs. Rosie Woodman show their letter to that nobody Hendersen, watch them tear up that contract he had on Hattie.

Seeing them packed up and ready to head Philadelphia way would put my heart through the gin, but I knew they'd be right happy up there, maybe even send me a letter or two. Why, Hattie could go to a regular old school. Miss Rosie could keep searching for her boys. And one of my letters would find Mr. Jonah's Rosie in Macon. It'd be right fine.

Almost as fine as Oak Grove would be, now that it had the folks owning it by God's right and man's right too. I couldn't wait no more to see it. Mr. Dooley hadn't even turned the horses up the drive before I pitched over the side, ran up to the office, climbed that woodpile, and had me a roost on that roof. Put my hands out to shout, "I'm home, thank the Lord, I'm home.

Did you love this book?

Want to get access to
the hottest books for free?

Log on to simonandschuster.com/pulseit
to find out how to join,
get access to cool sweepstakes,
and hear about your favorite authors!

Become part of Pulse IT and tell us what you think!